MW01016083

BLOW

BLOW

JODI LUNDGREN

James Lorimer & Company Ltd., Publishers
Toronto

James Lorimer & Company Ltd., Publishers acknowledges the support of the Ontario Arts Council. We acknowledge the financial support of the Government of Canada through the Canada Book Fund for our publishing activities. We acknowledge the support of the Canada Council for the Arts which last year invested $24.3 million in writing and publishing throughout Canada. We acknowledge the Government of Ontario through the Ontario Media Development Corporation's Ontario Book Initiative.

Cover design: Meredith Bangay
Cover image: Flickr

Library and Archives Canada Cataloguing in Publication

Lundgren, Jodi, 1966-, author
        Blow / Jodi Lundgren.

(SideStreets)
Issued in print and electronic formats.
ISBN   978-1-4594-0598-1   (pbk.).--ISBN   978-1-4594-0599-8
(bound).--ISBN 978-1-4594-0600-1 (epub)

    I. Title. II. Series: SideStreets

PS8573.U542B56 2014   jC813'.54   C2013-906777-9
C2013-906778-7

James Lorimer & Company Ltd.,   Distributed in the United States by:
Publishers   Orca Book Publishers
317 Adelaide Street West, Suite 1002   P.O. Box 468
Toronto, ON, Canada   Custer, WA USA
M5V 1P9   98240-0468
www.lorimer.ca

Printed and bound in Canada
Manufactured by Webcom in Toronto, Ontario in March 2014.
Job #411694

1

PHAT PIZZA

It's Friday night, and Phat Pizza is hopping when Julie and I walk in. Jeff Minh is working the counter. A few months ago, Jeff stopped being just one of the guys we hang out with. Now he's a hottie. Maybe it's the leather jacket he started to wear, or the way his face has slimmed down enough to let his square jawline show. Whatever it is, Julie's fallen hard. So far, he hasn't made a move.

He's talking across the counter to a girl in a halter top who's looking down at her own chest. Jeff's looking there too. Julie tenses up beside me. The fact is, she's got nothing to worry about. Her body is perfect, and she dresses a lot classier than that pathetic chick.

Jeff straightens up when he sees us and runs his hand through his hair.

Miss Look-at-my-Boobs drifts off, giggling and carrying a slice of pizza on a paper plate. Her stiletto heels force her to take baby steps. As she looks back over her shoulder at Jeff, she bumps into Julie.

Julie scowls. "Watch it!"

"So — rry!" The girl drags the word into two syllables. She bugs her blue eyes at me as if to say, "What's *her* problem?" She totters to the exit. At the door, she turns and wiggles the fingers of her free hand. "See you later, Jeff, honey!"

Julie rolls her shoulders back and struts up to the counter. "Friend of yours?" She tilts her head toward the door.

A slight flush travels up Jeff's cheeks. "Just a customer."

Julie flicks back her long, dark hair and leans forward on the counter, copying the other woman. "Looked like you were having a pretty intense talk." She shimmies her shoulders, then straightens up and laughs.

Jeff blushes deeper and looks away, but not before he takes in an eyeful of Julie's cleavage.

Julie has curves where I have angles. She acts sassy when I act shy. It's hard to get noticed around her. I need to get in on the conversation somehow. "What were you two talking about?"

Jeff presses his palms on the counter and shifts his weight. Then he looks straight at me and raises an eyebrow. "She was asking me what I thought of her boob job."

Julie snorts. "I knew they were fake!"

"What'd you tell her?" I ask.

Jeff flashes a plastic, customer-service smile. "Do you want that for here or to go?"

A grin plays around Julie's lips. Secretly, she likes it that Jeff works at such a popular place and that so many girls think he's hot enough to flirt with. But if flirting is a game — or a tournament, more like — she wants to knock out her opponents one by one until she wins the prize. The prize? Jeff. Me? I'm just the score-keeper. This round, Julie: 1. Boob Job: 0.

When I got dragged to this town — Red Deer, Alberta — from Vancouver last year, Julie was the only one in grade ten as short as I was, so I followed her around until she let me be her friend. Luckily, she belonged to a big group who let me hang with them, too. They weren't all Filipino Canadian like Julie, but I was basically the only white girl.

Jeff passes us each a paper plate that holds a slice of plain cheese pizza. "They're on me. Take a seat, and I'll stop by when I can get Lee to cover for me."

Lee and Jeff are cousins. They come from a pretty traditional Vietnamese family. Jeff's parents own the shop, and they run it as a family business. Now that Jeff's in grade twelve, he's the night manager. Lee's still working his way up.

We watch Jeff from our stools as we nibble our pizza. The customers are mostly drunk people spilling out of the nightclubs nearby. A group of four men swarms into the shop, yelling, "A whole pizza with extra spices for delivery!"

Julie looks at me. "Sucks that we got IDed." The expression on her face is so sour that it puckers her cheeks.

We're both in grade eleven now, but she repeated a year when her family first moved to Canada. That means she's nearly eighteen, the drinking age. She hardly ever gets IDed anymore. I'm only sixteen, and I look it. I can't get into a restricted movie, let alone a bar.

"I really wanted to go dancing tonight, Meringue."

At least she's still calling me by my nickname. If she were really annoyed, she'd use my real name, Mary. I got nicknamed after I joined Julie's crowd. At first, Jeff called me "Banana Cream Pie." Julie had to explain it to me: "It's because you hang out with us. It means you're white on the outside and yellow on the inside."

I didn't get it.

Julie rolled her eyes. "Asians who try to fit in with whites get called bananas. Don't you know anything? So you're the opposite."

Being surrounded by Asian kids was totally normal to me. In Vancouver, it wasn't something people made cracks about.

Then one day Julie came up with "Lemon Meringue Pie." She said, "Mary sounds kind of like Meringue."

Meringue has stuck as my nickname ever since.

Jeff slides onto the stool next to Julie and nods at me. A few strands of black hair curve over one eyebrow. "How are you two doing?"

She touches his arm. "Better now that you're here!" Her eyes glitter as she smiles at him.

She's coming on so strong. I could never be so . . . obvious. So confident. Then again, maybe if I had her assets, flirting would come naturally. Nothing seems to come naturally to me anymore. Jeff and I used to joke around, but now that he's become a Hot Stud, I can barely talk to him.

Jeff turns to me. "Like the pizza?"

First, I have to finish chewing. Then I have to swallow. Finally, I say, "Yeah. It's very . . . cheesy."

They laugh at my lame answer, and I duck my head. It's not like I didn't have time to think up a better one. I swear I used to be more witty. Maybe it's juvenile dementia setting in.

Jeff turns back to Julie. "I can get off after I make a delivery run."

"Really?" Julie purrs. "How long will that take?"

"Forty-five minutes, tops."

She can't hold back a groan of disappointment.

He nudges her leg with his knee. "Come on, it's not that long. When I get back, I'll buy you drinks."

She perks up at the mention of alcohol. "Does that mean we can go to the Elbow Room?" Lucky for Jeff, he turned eighteen in January.

"Sure. Meringue'll keep you company 'til I

get back. Right, Meringue?"

I roll my eyes in reply. If I had my driver's licence, I'd get out of here. Being a tagalong is getting old. It's been almost a year since I got my Learner's. In three weeks, if I practise enough, I can take the road test for my Class 5-Graduated Driver Licensing. With my Class 5-GDL, I can drive on my own. Mom has even promised to "car share" with me.

While we wait for Jeff, I flick my finger back and forth across the end of a paper match until it frays. I hold the head of the match and peel the base into strips. When I tried smoking, for about a week, the only part I liked was lighting up. So I still carry matches or a lighter, even though I don't smoke. It means I always have a light for friends, and I always have something to fidget with.

"Making another match person?" Julie acts like I'm a mentally challenged person doing art therapy. She taps her phone.

"Texting again?" I try to match her mocking tone. She thinks texting is much better than what I'm doing, but it's about as exciting to watch. I like hanging out at Julie's way better than this. She has all these younger siblings, and the house buzzes with life in a way I never got to experience as an only child. It makes me feel like I belong to something bigger.

Julie looks at her phone and shakes her head. "My Mom. Reminding me to be home by midnight. Or else."

Julie likes to sleep over at my house because it gives her a break from babysitting. Besides, Mom is much more liberal than her parents. We can watch shows that her parents don't approve of and stay up as late as we want.

A customer storms in carrying a pizza box. He yells at Lee, who's on cash. "Where are the extra spices, man?"

"I put them in there, on the side, like you asked." Lee looks over his shoulder, but no one pops out of the kitchen to save him from this loud guy who's built like a hockey player. He probably works on the oil rigs.

I pick up the glass shaker of hot spices from our table and carry it to the counter.

"Here, you can use ours."

Lee nods and points to the jar. Rig guy glances down at me, not getting it. "What is this shit?"

"I think it's dried jalapeño and pimento flakes."

He shakes his head back and forth fast, like he just got out of a swimming pool. "Okay, joke's over. Where's Jeff?"

Lee says, "He's making deliveries."

Rig guy slams the pizza box on the counter. "Then fuckin' give me my money back."

I've never seen someone try to return a takeout pizza. Lee swallows and looks at the box. He moves to the cash register. His hands are shaking as he counts out the bills.

Rig guy yells again. "*All* of my money, you little shit!"

Lee jumps back from the counter. "I gave it to you!"

"What the . . .? Oh, p-lease." The man

reaches between the tip jar and the cash register. It looks as if he snatches a couple of bills. "You can tell Jeff I'm taking my business elsewhere!" He stomps out and slams the door.

Lee pokes his head into the kitchen and stands there. He must be talking to the cook. When he returns to the cash, I approach him. "That dude was a real a-hole."

Lee raises his eyebrows and nods. "We've been getting some real pricks in here lately. I hate doing this shift. The cook thinks we should get Uncle Thuan to install a security camera."

"And maybe one of those buttons that you can step on to call the cops."

A couple of girls come up behind me to order, so I move off to the side.

"Meringue —"

I turn my head back toward Lee.

"What?"

A warm smile opens up his face. "Thanks for trying to help."

Trying to help. I know he doesn't mean it like that, but it's true. I was *actually* no help at all. Story of my life. I force myself to smile back at Lee, anyway. "Sure."

Julie frowns as I make my way back to our table. "What was that all about?"

I shrug. "Unhappy customer, I guess."

"He sure let everyone know about it! It gave me goosebumps when he yelled." Julie rubs one arm and then the other with her opposite hand.

"You want to take off?"

"And ditch Jeff?" Julie widens her eyes at me.

"It's not like we had plans with him tonight." I lower my voice. "I mean, we're basically stalking him."

Julie slams both palms on the table. If she were a cartoon character, steam would pour out of her ears. "I am *not* a stalker, Meringue! Jeff is always saying, 'Hey, drop by the shop tonight; I'm working.' He's invited me so many times, and I never come. I felt bad!

Tonight I finally broke down and came." She slumps back on her stool. "Geez."

I bite my lip. "Sorry." I have to say something to smooth things over. "I feel like a third wheel. I mean, you and Jeff are so perfect for each other, and I'm just tagging along."

Julie's eyes flash, then a shadow crosses them. "You really think we're perfect for each other?" Her voice quavers. She sounds way less sure of herself than I thought she was.

"Of course you are! I mean, you're both so incredibly good looking, and you're almost the same age." It hits me how shallow those reasons sound. I try to think up some deeper ones. "You've been friends for ages, and lately it seems like you really pay attention to what the other person is saying." I sit up straight, trying to look more convincing. "That shows you care."

Julie nods and then tilts her chin up. "But did you see the way he blushed when we teased him about that older chick? I think he might really be into her."

I picture the way Jeff cocked an eyebrow at me when he mentioned the "boob job." He wasn't taking that woman seriously at all. "He was just embarrassed. It doesn't mean he's into her."

She sighs and tugs her blouse straight. "I hope you're right. I mean, he graduates in June. I've still got another year. Maybe he doesn't want to get stuck with some high-school kid."

It's weird that Julie wants me to reassure her. She's the one who's had boyfriends before. But with other guys, she always had the upper hand. This time, she's met her match. Jeff seems to like her, but he's playing it cool.

As for me — well, what do my feelings matter? Jeff's way out of my league, and the faster I get over my crush on him, the better. He and Julie would be a much better pair.

Jeff breezes back in carrying the empty pizza delivery bag. "Thanks for waiting, you guys."

Julie bats her eyelashes. "Are we still going to the Elbow Room?"

Jeff steps up to her and slings his arm around her shoulders. "A promise is a promise!" He looks at me. "Coming, Meringue?"

"I can't get in there." For the first time, I'm glad I look too young to pass. This way, I don't have to watch Julie and Jeff flirt all night.

"Too bad." He lets his arm slide off Julie's shoulders. "I should give you a ride home, then."

There's no way I want them to give me a ride. It would just rub it in that I'm the little kid who has to get home to bed, so the big kids can hit the town. I check my phone: 10:45 p.m. Buses are still running to Michener Hill. "It's okay." I slide off my stool and zip up my coat.

"Are you sure?" Jeff lifts his eyebrows. "It's no problem."

I look straight at him. "Positive. But thanks, anyway."

Julie's face lights up, but she holds herself back from smiling too big. "Later, Meringue.

I'll call you!"

It's not like the streets are deserted. People are milling around everywhere. I head north on Gaetz to Sorensen Station, the downtown hub for buses. It's raining, so I pull up my hood and stick my hands in my pockets. I check the schedule that's inside a plastic square attached to a pole. Fifteen minutes to wait. I pace up and down to keep warm.

That's when I notice the other people pacing in front of the station. They're mostly wearing hoodies, like me, but they look a lot older. The men have whiskers, and the women have acne scabs. One of the men sidles up to me. "You look new."

"I'm not new. I just don't usually ride the bus."

His eyes seem to be all pupil. After a long pause, he reacts. "Don't usually ride the bus. Ha! Good one. The magic bus, eh?"

He's freaking me out, so I cross the street and head up 49th Avenue toward the next bus stop. Someone else veers into me. "Are you looking for something?" His voice is so low, he practically croaks.

"No!" I speed up my walk.

He shouts, "Hey!" after me.

These weirdos are enough to turn me off going downtown at night. I can't wait to get my licence. When I share the car, I'll just climb in, lock the doors, and drive home — safe and sound.

I cover three or four blocks before a bus comes up behind me. I hop on. I don't even care if it's the right bus or not. Any direction is okay, as long as it's away from downtown.

2

SCOOTER

On Saturday morning, I take a long bike ride on the paved trail beside the Red Deer River. It's that time of year between winter and spring, when the ice is turning to slush. This is the first weekend that it has looked safe to bike again. On the trail, I pass only a few other cyclists. Chunks of ice still line the riverbanks, but the water is flowing. Riding makes me feel so free. This is how it's going to feel when I get my driver's licence. Only better. I'll be able to go farther and faster, and bring my friends along. My lungs burn and so do my cheeks. I ride all the way along the south side of the river to Heritage Ranch and then double back.

When I get home, a scooter is parked in our carport. It has shiny red panels, sleek handle-bars, and a black faux-leather seat. Mom's car isn't there. *Have I got the wrong unit?* Hard to believe. We've lived here for over a year. I count in from the end of the row of town-houses: one, two, three, four. No, this one is definitely ours.

From the carport, I open the door into the house. In the mud room, someone in a white space suit is standing with their back to me. Okay, the space suit is really a white jacket with black and grey stripes down the left-hand side. Two legs inside matching pants fork below the jacket. The person wearing the suit spins around when I shut the door.

Mom gushes. "What do you think? Isn't the scooter gorgeous? Like a sculpture on wheels."

"Is this going to be like the time you bought a kayak and never used it?" I brush past her and raid the kitchen cupboards for a snack.

She follows me. "No, Mary. This time I'll definitely use it."

"How can you be so sure?"

"I won't have much choice after trading in the car!"

I stop dead and whirl around with a box of rice crackers in my hand. "You're trading. In. The car?"

"I don't think we really need it, do you? The scooter carries two."

"I'm supposed to take my road test in three weeks, remember? You said you were going to car share!"

Mom's face falls a bit. "We can share the scooter, too."

"But how am I going to practise for my test? You said you'd take me out driving when the snow melted. Well, look around. It's gone!"

She gasps and covers her mouth with her hand. "Honey, I'm sorry." She holds still for a moment and then drops her hands to her sides. "The truth is, this move has been more expensive than I bargained for." She looks at the floor and lowers her voice. "We need the cash."

"Are you serious?" I can't believe my mother. It's almost like she's never grown up.

She hangs her head. "I'm sorry, Mary. I'm hoping it's only temporary." Then she cheers up. "But you'll have six weeks with your dad this summer. He'd love to help you. And he's a much better driver than I am."

I clench my jaw. "If I have my Class 5 *before* the summer, then I can drive in Vancouver. I can go places with my friends! None of them can drive on their own 'til they're seventeen. You know that!"

When my parents split up in March of last year, Mom had the urge to move back to her home town of Red Deer. Population 95,000. Also known as Dead Rear, for good reason. I wanted to stay in Vancouver, so Mom used the licensing laws as a bribe. In Alberta, you can get your Learner's at fourteen. And at sixteen, after passing the road test, you can drive on your own and have passengers. Problem is, Mom won't take me out to practise driving during the winter, and in the summer, I visit my dad. Last year, Dad refused to drive with me because I was underage in B.C. But he said when I'm sixteen and have a Class 5-GDL, I'll be legal. He won't try to stop me.

She touches my arm. "How about learning to ride a scooter? Come on. Let's take it for a test ride. I brought a helmet for you."

She hands me a pair of gloves and a silver helmet with an eye shield. Before I have time to finish my snack, she hustles me back out the door. She grabs the handlebars and straddles the scooter. I don't move, and she twists to look at me. "What are you waiting for? Come on!"

I'm still mad at her, but I'm sort of curious about the scooter. It's a motorized vehicle, after all. I sling my leg across the seat behind her.

"Just hang onto my waist and lean into the turns."

And just like that, we're riding. She picks

the least trafficky roads she can find — residential streets where kids are shooting hoops and old folks are working in the yard. She yells over her shoulder, "I want to go somewhere where we can pick up some speed!"

That's how we end up whipping along country roads, the wind on our faces. On a map of Alberta, you can practically draw a vertical line from Edmonton down to Calgary. Stop halfway, and you hit Red Deer. We're ninety minutes away from a major city in either direction. But we're not heading north or south. Highway 11A heads due west. We pass one farm after another. Not counting the flat countryside and the poker-straight road, the ride reminds me of the "field trips" we used to take in Vancouver when I was homeschooling. Mom was always sweeping me off to an exhibit at the museum or to a children's symphony concert or to a mother-daughter belly dance class.

She pushes the scooter to its maximum speed, around 70 clicks. She should really have bought a motorbike. Every so often a truck zooms up and pulls around us to pass. One guy honks and jerks his thumb at Mom as if to say, "Get to the side of the road!" The next guy honks and tips his cowboy hat at her with a leer. After nearly half an hour, we reach a roundabout, continue straight through, and head on to where a lake stretches out in front of us, grey and still. Wet patches glisten on the surface of the lake, which means the ice is melting. We hang a right and follow the lakeshore until the road merges back into the highway. Just as I'm wondering if Mom has any idea where she's going, a road sign appears: Jarvis Bay Provincial Campground. She pulls in and brakes. I slide to my feet.

She dismounts, holding the scooter upright. "Your turn!"

Only a couple of cars dot the parking lot. "Are you sure?"

"Why not?"

I shrug. At least the snow has melted. "I hope you've got good insurance."

Mom stands beside me while I mount the bike. I place one foot on the ground and one on the deck to get a feel for the scooter's weight. It's a lot like a bike, especially because of the hand brakes. The thick gloves make my hands feel clumsy. But I squeeze the brake and press the starter button with my thumb. The engine revs.

"Put both feet up. I'll hold you." Mom steps in close, supports the handlebars, and pushes the kickstand with her toe. "Twist the right handle to accelerate. Ready?"

I release the brake and give it some gas. The scooter lunges forward. I'm riding! I ease back on the accelerator and circle the lot. The gravel makes for a bumpy ride, but steering is easier than I expected. I loop back to Mom and brake.

"Great job!" she says. "How about driving into the campground?"

"Huh?"

She points to the end of the parking lot where a road opens up. "That's the way to the campsites. Let me get on behind you."

Doubling, it's hard to find my balance at first.

With her arms around me, Mom calls out encouraging words. I circle the lot a few times until we stop wobbling. Then I nose the scooter onto the dirt road. The road zigzags in wide curlicues through a forest, getting closer and closer to the lake. Tucked into the trees are bare patches of earth, each with a picnic table and a fire pit. Just when I'm getting the hang of turning corners, the engine stutters and cuts out. The fuel gauge reads Empty. I coast to a stop. "Now what?"

Turns out the tank holds only five litres of gas, and it was nowhere near full when we set out.

"Great." I climb off the scooter and fold my arms over my chest.

Mom pats her pockets. "Do you have your phone? Mine's in my other coat."

I hand over my cell, and she calls her boyfriend, Steve. "We're out at Sylvan Lake," she says.

So *that's* where we are. He agrees to rescue us in his pickup truck, but it'll take him at least half an hour.

Mom and I each take a handlebar and push the scooter up the path. "Quite an adventure, huh?" Mom sounds way too chipper. If I respond, it'll only encourage her. Our feet scuff the cold earth as we trudge up the path.

Back in the parking lot, there's still a long wait. My jacket is thinner than Mom's, so I jog in circles to stay warm. By the time Steve finally pulls up in his black truck, I'm starving.

Steve grins at my Mom like it's the cutest thing to get stranded miles away from the nearest gas station. I bet that smile would fade pretty quickly if she traded in his truck without telling him. I almost blurt out, "The honeymoon won't last! She'll drive you crazy!" But I catch myself. I don't want to scare him off. Mom seems happier since she met him. The last thing I want is for her to go back to crying in front of a movie every night.

Steve hoists the scooter into the back of his truck and anchors it down with bungee cords. Mom climbs onto the flatbed and tries to help, but mostly just gets in the way. When

Steve's done, he vaults back out of the truck. His work boots land with a crunch on the gravel. He wipes his hands on his jeans. Then he turns and stretches a hand out to Mom. She takes it and steps over the tailgate. Balanced on the bumper, she puts her hands on Steve's shoulders while he holds her waist. "Thanks for bailing us out, Steve." She gets all gooey-eyed. "I don't know what we would have done without you." They look into each other's eyes as she hops to the ground.

I don't ever want to rely on a guy the way Mom does. When I get my licence, I'll definitely sign up for a roadside assistance plan.

Steve hugs her. "No problem, babe." He tousles her hair. "But maybe you should get a model with a reserve fuel tank?"

"No, I like this one!" she says. "Besides, the sale is already final."

The words slice through me like a cold wind. "It *is*?" I put my hands on my hips and glare at her. Up until now, I didn't really believe she would sell the car. I thought this was just a test ride. I was sure she wouldn't go back on her promise to car share with me.

Mom flashes me a look that says, "We'll talk later."

I'm so angry that riding in the back of the truck seems better than sitting in the cab beside Mom. Steve talks me out of it. "You'll freeze, sweetie."

It's a tight squeeze in the front seat between Mom's armoured jacket and Steve's bulky frame. Steve cranks the heat. He reaches under the seat and pulls out a box of granola bars. They're a boring oat-and-honey flavour, but I wolf down two of them. My mind churns as fast as my jaws. Since Mom sold the car, there's only one thing to do.

Buy my own vehicle. One that won't get sold out from under me. One that will always be there when I need it. One that is mine.

3

A JOB

Online, I check my bank balance: $471.03. It's not bad considering I've saved it up through birthday money and babysitting jobs. On Auto Trader, there's one car, a Ford Taurus, listed for $500. I'm excited until I read the description. It's got almost 300,000 kilometres on it, and Dad said to stay away from cars with more than 200,000 kilometres. After I've clicked around, it looks like $1,500 is going to be closer to a reasonable price. Then there's insurance. Suddenly, buying a car is looking further away.

Bzzz. A text arrives on my phone. *Come down at 4. Discards!!*

Julie works at a clothing store in the mall. Every so often, the staff is allowed to scoop up leftover merchandise. Sale items that didn't move and aren't considered worth the cost of return shipping. Mutant garments with missing buttons or uneven sleeves. Julie doesn't usually take the discards. She uses her staff discount to buy clothes when they're brand new and trending. But she likes to act as my stylist. And I don't mind the free clothes.

I bike to the mall and get there just before Julie gets off her shift. She's helping a lady accessorize a grey dress. She slips her a red belt, a patterned scarf, a pair of shoes. As a final touch, she slides the woman's arms into a dark-grey blazer. The lady is studying herself in a mirror when Julie's manager walks by and compliments her. It's true that the outfit looks good. It's also a pretty slick operation. The customer checks her watch and says, "Look at the time! Okay, I'll take it. All of it."

Julie gives the customer a polite smile, but when she steals a glance at her manager, her eyes shine like she just won the lottery. She'll get a hefty commission from this transaction.

After she rings up the sale, Julie ushers me into the back. "Here they are! I thought of you right away."

A collection of evening gowns hangs on a rack. My wardrobe consists mostly of hoodies and jeans. So the dresses don't really scream "me," to say the least.

"If you wore one of these dresses, with the right heels and makeup, I bet I could get you into the Elbow Room."

She guides me into a dressing room and hangs up the clothes on a hook. Then she backs out of the cubicle and shuts the curtain.

I unzip my hoodie and step out of my jeans. "How was it last night?"

"It was okay."

I slide a red dress off its hanger. "Only okay?" I pull it over my head and then yank open the curtain. "Can you zip this up?"

Julie works on the zipper. We both look at my reflection in the mirror. The dress hangs loose and baggy in the bust. She frowns. "Try the blue one."

The blue one has a zipper on the side, so I don't need help to get it on. That's a plus. But it's just as baggy in the chest as the first one.

"Damn!" Julie says. "These are extra-smalls. I thought for sure they would fit you."

"Face it. You need a rack for these dresses."

"The black one is cut differently. Try it on."

I step back into the change room and close the curtain. "So, did you dance at the Elbow Room?" I shimmy out of the blue dress and into the black one.

On the other side of the curtain, Julie sighs. "There was no dancing. Jeff bought me a Long Island Iced Tea and then these other guys came up to him. Ten minutes later, he said we had to go. I had to pound back my drink. He drove me straight home, acting all distracted. He wouldn't tell me what was going on. He didn't even hug me goodbye. Just said he'd call. And he hasn't."

"It was only last night, Jules. Give him twenty-four hours, at least."

The black dress is stretchy. It hugs my body a little more closely. I open the curtain.

"That's better!" Julie says.

In the mirror, the neckline of the dress plunges to my sternum. "I can't wear this!"

"Why not?"

"Look how low-cut it is."

Julie snorts. "It's sophisticated."

"It's indecent."

"If you show a little more skin, you look older."

Problem is, I don't look older. I look like a little girl playing dress-up in her Mom's closet. The only thing that's going to make me seem older is a car. Not this dress. But it's free, and Julie's trying to be nice. "Okay, I'll take it. Thanks."

She smiles. "Great. I'll wrap it up. Then let's hit the food court. I'm starving."

***

"Stupid rain." Julie looks out the window at the drops hitting the sidewalk. "I'll get soaked on the way home."

"Me, too." I take a sip of pop. I saved my money and didn't buy any food. "Sure be nice to have a car."

"My dad won't even let me get my Learner's," Julie fumes. "He thinks it'll just encourage me to find an older boyfriend to drive around with!"

Julie's dad has a point. Any eighteen-year-old with a licence can supervise a learner.

"And I need parental consent to get it," she continues. "My mom won't go against my dad. So I'm screwed."

I gaze at Julie's plate of fries, and my mouth waters. "I'm screwed too."

"You?" She dips a fry in ketchup. "You're getting your licence in three weeks! You keep telling me."

"Mom just sold the car. I'm going to have

to buy one for myself if I want to drive."

Julie rounds her eyes. "You're going to buy a car?"

"I want to. But I don't have the money."

She shrugs. "Get a job!"

Across the food court, a few guys enter as a pack. Their jet black hair makes them easy to pick out. It's our friends from school. Jeff stands a head and shoulders above the rest. He scans the court, spots us, and says something to the others. They wave to us and get in line at a burger stand as Jeff makes his way over.

"Long time no see!" he jokes. "What's up?"

Julie doesn't smile. "Just finished my shift."

"Sorry I had to bail last night, Julie," he says. "We keep getting slammed at work. It's hard for me to take any time off."

She shrugs and looks at her plate.

He leans on the back of the empty chair in front of me. "What are you up to, Meringue?"

I arch an eyebrow at Julie. "Job hunting, I guess."

"Yeah?" He keeps glancing over at Julie,

trying to catch her eye. "What kind of work are you looking for?" He's just asking to be polite.

But before I can answer, he does a double take. It's like he's seeing me for the very first time and noticing something important about me. "Wait, I could totally use you!"

I slap a hand to my chest. "Me?"

Eyes wide, he keeps staring. "I need someone to help out with deliveries. Someone I can trust with my car. How about it?"

Julie's mouth falls open.

I splutter. "I've only got my Learner's."

"When can you take your road test?"

"In three weeks, technically. But there's no way I can be ready. My mom just sold the car."

Jeff reaches across the table and puts his hand on my shoulder. "I could take you out." His fingers feel cool through my shirt. He lowers his voice. "I just can't keep doing it all by myself."

Julie folds her arms across her chest and glares at me.

"Why me?" I say.

Jeff hesitates for a minute. He glances over his shoulder at our friends in line at the burger stand. "The guys — they all have jobs. And we need my cousin Lee out front."

Then I think of something. "Even if I get my Class 5-GDL, I'll still be probationary."

Jeff winks at me. "Perks of being a night manager," he says. "It doesn't matter to me. The main thing is you can legally drive on your own after that."

There must be plenty of fully licensed drivers Jeff could hire — even ones who have their own cars. He shifts to stand behind me and massages both my shoulders. His touch makes my cheeks feel hot. "Think about it, okay? It's like I said." He ducks down to look me in the eye. "I need someone I can trust."

Julie frowns at her plate.

"Later, you two!" Jeff cuts through the crowds and catches up with the others just as they're placing their orders.

Julie balls up her napkin and throws it on the table. "I'm out of here."

***

At home, I search the kitchen for something I can cook for myself. Mom comes in and stands in the doorway with her arms crossed. "Steve invited us both out for dinner."

I turn my back to her and squat to look in the cupboards. "No thanks."

A box of macaroni and cheese sits on the shelf. I grab it. I fill up a pan with water from the tap and set it on the burner to boil.

Mom is still leaning against the door jamb, watching me.

"What?" I ask.

"I'm sorry about the car. I should have talked it over with you."

I'm not about to let her off the hook. "That's for sure! Plus, I can't see how you're going to manage on that thing in the winter. I suppose you expect Steve to drive you around." I tear open the box of macaroni. "First you force me to leave all my friends and move here with you, and now you take away the car. I'm sick of you wrecking my life!"

"Oh, honey." Mom's face twists up like she's about to cry. "I'm sorry."

"Never mind." I rip open the packet of cheese powder, and orange crystals fly across the stove top. "I'm going to save up and buy my own car."

She gulps and nods. "Good for you."

I can tell she's not taking me seriously. "I already have a job offer."

"Really?" Mom says. "Are you sure you want to take on a job on top of your school work? Why don't you wait until summer?"

"You had an after-school job when you were my age!"

"I know, but that's because my family wasn't well off. I didn't want to be working. I wanted to hang out and be a kid."

I fling my arms out to the sides, palms turned up. "We're not well off, either!"

Mom's shoulders sag.

"Anyway, I'm sick of being a kid. All my friends here have jobs."

Mom sighs and sinks sideways into a kitchen chair, one elbow propped on the back of it. "So who made you the offer?"

"Jeff." I'm proud to say it. "He's the night manager at Phat Pizza."

"The night manager? You'd have to work nights? Where is Phat Pizza?"

"The corner of 47th and Gaetz."

"Downtown!" Mom shakes her head. "I don't know about this, Mary."

"What do you mean, you 'don't know'? I didn't ask you!"

She takes a deep breath. "I guess as long as he's not asking you to make deliveries . . ."

I turn back to the stove and place a lid on the pot of water.

"Mary. He's not asking you to make deliveries, is he?"

I keep my eyes on the stove. "We didn't discuss the details, Mom. There are a lot of different jobs in a pizza shop, you know. Someone has to be on cash, someone has to handle the phone orders, they need people in the kitchen . . ."

I glance over my shoulder. Mom is staring into space and nodding. "Right. Well, maybe it will be okay. I'm sure he wouldn't let you work as a driver without your full licence."

The burner glows red. Guilt twists in my stomach. The water is taking forever to boil.

4

DRIVING LESSON

Bzzz. Bzzz. My bedside clock says 9:30 a.m., which means Julie must have some life-or-death news. If she's not working, Julie usually sleeps 'til noon on the weekend. The morning light hurts, so I clench my eyes shut, reach out from under the covers, and grope the night-stand for my phone.

I press buttons to open the new message. One eye cracks open just far enough to read it: *Why don't we take a spin today?*

Is she joking? Or does she mean she wants a ride on the scooter? Either way, it's not funny. I'm about to text her when I notice the sender's name.

It's not Julie.

It's Jeff!

I sit up in bed and tug down the T-shirt that I sleep in. I finger comb my hair. Tangles catch on my knuckles before they give way. Jeff hardly ever texts me. The memory of his hands massaging my shoulders makes me flush.

I reread the text. He's not asking about the scooter. He's asking about practising for my driving test. Before I can figure out how to respond, the phone buzzes again.

How soon can u be ready?

My heart is pounding, and I'm wide awake. My fingers tap the keys. *½ hr?* As soon as I send it, I regret it. I should have said an hour.

K. C u soon!

I jump into the shower. Usually, the warm water pelting my back relaxes me. So does the lavender scent of my shower gel. But my shoulders are tensing up. Jeff and I never hang out one-on-one. It's giving me the jitters.

As I dry off with my favourite fluffy towel, another text sounds. My heart beats faster. Damn! I can't ever let Jeff know the effect he has on me. *Must calm down.* I wrap the towel around me and cross the hall to my bedroom. The message light pulses on my phone. I take a breath and tap the screen.

On my way!

If this were happening to some other girl — someone like Julie — I'd think the guy liked her and had come up with a smart way to spend time with her. But it's Jeff — hot, confident, older Jeff — and me, flat-chested, tongue-tied, sixteen-year-old me. I can't figure it out. Maybe once he sees how rusty my driving skills are, he'll change his mind.

Drying my hair takes time. I pull on my best jeans and shrug into a magenta hoodie with sheepskin lining. In the kitchen, there's no sign of Mom, but voices are murmuring behind her bedroom door down the hall. I yank open the curtains. Steve's truck sits in the driveway. I leave Mom a note on the counter.

Gone to practise driving with Jeff. Back later.

***

"It's been quite the weekend." I buckle into the passenger seat of Jeff's dark-grey Honda Civic. "First my mom teaches me to ride a scooter and now this."

He shoots me a smile. He's wearing a faded green sweatshirt under a black ski jacket, and he smells like Ivory soap. A few strands of his hair glisten, damp from the shower. "Best place to practise is the college. Lots of parking lots and not many people around on a Sunday."

My stomach growls. I blow-dried my hair instead of eating breakfast.

He laughs. "Want to grab a bite on the way? I could use a coffee."

We take Gaetz to the south side of town. Two lanes head south, but there's not much traffic on a Sunday morning. Red Deer's a sprawling city of one-storey plazas with only the occasional high-rise. Normally, the horizon stretches as far as the eye can see. But just before we get to Tim Hortons, there's a crest in the road that I can't see over. It makes me curious. If I were driving, I'd keep going just to see what's on the other side.

But, instead, we turn off the road at a Super 8 motel that shares a parking lot with Timmys. As I get out of the car, a faint scent of pine fills the air. Across the street, the evergreens of Rotary Park stand tall. Last fall, I biked all the way there on the Waskasoo Trails. One good thing about moving from a big city to a small one is that it doesn't take long to learn your way around.

Jeff holds the door for me, and I walk in ahead of him. People wearing turquoise scrubs fill a couple of tables. The hospital is only a block away. At the counter, a girl from our school stands waiting in a brown uniform and cap. Her eyes dart back and forth between me and Jeff. We've hung out lots of times, but we've always been part of a pack. No one has ever sized us up like that.

"Stacy, how's it goin'?" he says.

They chat about some homework that's due tomorrow in Biology. Jeff's an A student — he wants to be a dentist — and he gives her some tips. My eyes rove the donut display, and my mouth is watering when Jeff says, "Do you know Meringue?"

"Huh?" Stacy says.

"Mary," I say. I hope she'll let it go at that. It's not always easy explaining why I was nicknamed after a pie.

A line has formed behind us, so Stacy lets it drop and takes our orders. "Is this separate or together?"

I pat my pocket to check for my wallet. My jacket is flat and empty against my ribs. In all the excitement, I forgot to bring money. *Damn*. I'm about to say something when

Jeff says, "Together."

Stacy's eyes flick back and forth between us some more as she gives Jeff his change. Does she think we're *together* together? "See you tomorrow, Jeff. Nice meeting you, uh, Mary."

Jeff sips his coffee and watches the staff behind the counter as we wait for our food. "Crazy. Only two people working at a peak time. We've got such a labour shortage in this town." He winks at me over his cup. "That's why I need you so bad."

I almost choke on my coffee. *Is he flirting with me?*

The only flavour I can identify in the breakfast sandwich is salt. I've lost my appetite, anyway. My stomach is churning.

From Timmys, it's a five-minute drive west to Red Deer College. As Jeff promised, the huge parking lots are mostly deserted. He parks, and we switch seats. The first thing I do is crank the driver's seat up as high as it will go. Then I yank it closer to the steering wheel and the pedals. I touch the stick shift.

Thank God, this is an automatic.

"Make sure you put the mirrors where you need them," Jeff says. He shows me how to adjust the side mirrors mechanically, and I fiddle with the rear-view by hand. "Okay, I think you're ready. Lights, camera, action!"

The basics come back to me pretty fast. Mom made me take lessons when I got my Learner's, even though she didn't take me out to practise very much. I drive around and around the lot. Jeff tells me I should practise parking, so I square the wheels of the car with the painted lines and pull in. Then I back out again. To mix it up, I back into a spot and drive forward out of it. I manage to avoid hitting the lampposts.

"You're doing great!" Jeff says. "We'll save parallel parking for another time. You want to drive on the road?"

"I don't think so. I need to go over the rules."

"Come on, just drive around College Circle. The only thing you're going to see is a stop sign." When I don't reply, he says, "Let's go over the rules. What do you do when you see a stop sign?"

I tuck my chin into my jacket and give an embarrassed laugh.

"Come on, Meringue, raise your hand if you know the answer."

I swat him, and he grabs my hand. "Very good, you raised your hand. I'll just hang onto it 'til you give the right answer."

Jeff's hand covers mine completely. His fingers feel warm, but they're clamping mine tight. It's a bit painful.

"Ow," I say.

He loosens his grip right away. I could pull my hand away, but I don't. "You wanted to review the rules of the road," he says. "I'm only trying to help."

All I'm aware of is my hand in his. It turns my brain to mush.

"So?" Jeff says.

"So what?"

"Want to drive around College Circle?"

"Okay."

"On which side of the road?" Jeff squeezes my hand.

His question makes me laugh. "On the right."

Jeff raises my hand to the roof of the car like I just won a boxing match. "That's right, champ! Go get 'em!"

I steer us out of the parking lot without crashing, but a few metres into the loop, the wheels thud against something and the car lurches. I slam on the brakes.

"Chill out!" Jeff says. "It's just a speed bump." He pats my thigh. "Just press the brake, don't stomp on it."

Every fifty metres or so, another speed bump jolts us. But before long, I can handle them.

"Now, try picking up the speed just a bit," Jeff says. "Nothing crazy. Just try going 30 instead of 20."

Being behind the wheel is growing on me. "Sure."

I'm cruising along at 30 clicks when Jeff yells, "Stop!"

I brake hard, and we're thrown forward against our seat belts. Just to the right of the car, a jogger runs on the spot, glaring in at me.

Jeff waves her through. "Shit. That was close."

"But there's no stop sign!"

He points to the zebra stripes of white paint on the road in front of us. The jogger gives me one last look before she crosses. "Pedestrians have the right of way," Jeff says. "Stop sign or not. She probably has an iPod under her hoodie. She didn't even see us 'til the brakes squealed."

My knuckles are white and my forearms are shaking. I shift into park and unbuckle my seat belt. "Quitting time."

"Really?"

But I'm already out the driver's side door, and this time he doesn't push it. He meets me beside the passenger door. "You did great, Meringue. Don't let a little mistake throw you. We'll practise again soon, alright?"

I shrug. "I guess so."

"Attagirl." He folds me into a hug, and it feels like I'm melting into his arms. I turn my head sideways and press my cheek against his chest. His heartbeat sounds in my ear. Before I can make a bigger fool of myself, he breaks the hold. He scoots around the car and into the driver's seat.

5

JULIE'S PLACE

Julie invites me over after school. She's supposed to take care of her younger brother and sisters 'til her parents get home from work. Even if they don't bring friends, it's always a full house. Busy and cheerful. The opposite of mine.

We walk from the high school to pick up the four-year-old, Piper, from daycare. He grabs Julie's hand with a big grin stretched across his face. "Julie, guess what we did today?"

Looking at me over his head, Julie rolls her eyes. She has to play this game every day. But her voice sounds excited. "Did you fly to the moon?"

Piper stops to consider this and then shakes his head. "No. Not today."

"Did you ride alligators down the river?"

Piper looks horrified. "Nooo!"

"Did you set the classroom on fire at nap time, when everyone else was asleep?"

I break in. "Don't give him ideas."

Piper grins. "Not today!"

"I give up, Piper. What did you do today?"

Piper tells a long story about his day that lasts until we get to the Catholic elementary school that Julie's sisters go to. Julie's parents let her switch into the public school system in grade nine because the Catholic high is so far south. In the schoolyard, her two sisters are playing tag with some other kids. Eight-year-old Paloma and ten-year-old Angie run fast in their stretch jeans and boots. Their long black hair ripples behind them. They keep running even when they leave the schoolyard. They outstrip us all the way home.

The kids ditch their gear on the floor of the mud room. "Hey! Hang up your coats!" Julie shakes her head at me. "They're spoiled. Mom always picks up after them."

She lifts Piper up onto the kitchen stool. For his snack, she cuts up an apple and makes a face with the slices on the plate. She uses raisins for the eyes. Paloma and Angie pour themselves glasses of milk and ask for banana bread.

"We finished it yesterday," Julie says. "How about a bowl of cereal?"

"No! Banana bread!" The girls cry in unison.

Piper chimes in. "Banana bwead!"

"Let's make more!" Angie says.

"Let's make more!" Paloma echoes.

Julie grabs the fruit bowl. It holds a couple of shrivelled apples and nothing else. "There are no bananas, see?"

Angie says, "Mom put some in the freezer."

Julie grimaces. "Really?"

Angie opens the freezer and grabs a black-skinned bunch of frozen bananas. It's one of the least-appetizing sights I've ever seen.

"Okay, you win. Let's make some banana bread." Out of the side of her mouth, Julie says, "It'll keep them out of trouble for awhile, anyway."

Julie's parents set strict limits on screen time, which makes babysitting a lot more work. The kids don't just disappear into their bedrooms to play video games or watch TV. Julie has to find things for them to do. While she supervises the banana-mashing, I build a fort out of cushions in the living room with Piper. He hides in his den with a blanket for a door and roars out to surprise me every so often. "Agh! A wild lion! That gave me a heart attack!" I roll onto my back and clutch my chest.

While the bread is baking, Paloma and Angie drift into the living room to play with Piper. I slip out to find Julie wiping flour off the counter. "I've got to wash up these dishes. Mom hates coming home to a messy kitchen when she has to make dinner."

"I'll dry."

Julie and I stand side by side at the sink, looking out the kitchen window. She plunges her hands wrist-deep into the soapy water. I finger tiny squares on the dish towel that look like they've been stamped on with a waffle iron. So far, I haven't told Julie about driving with Jeff. If I leave it much longer, she'll be mad at me for keeping secrets. Problem is, she might be jealous. She sure was frosty at the mall when he talked about hiring me as a driver.

"Stacy says you and Jeff were in Timmys yesterday."

It's like being shocked with static electricity. But I shouldn't be surprised. Most girls at school live to gossip. "It must be true, then."

Julie attacks the mixing bowl with the dish cloth. "What were you doing there?"

"You mean she didn't tell you what we ordered? I bet you know how many creams we had in our coffee."

Julie tosses the mixing bowl into the rinsing half of the sink, splashing me. "That's not what I mean."

I dip the bowl in the rinsing water and shake off the drops. In the window, I glimpse Julie's reflection. She's looking down, lips in a pout, shoulders slumped. The other night, her voice really trembled when she talked about Jeff. I soften my voice. "He wants me to take my Class 5 road test. So he took me out to practise driving."

"Hmph." Julie rinses banana pulp off the masher. "Stacy said he paid."

"That's only because I forgot my wallet." I swallow. I think that's the truth. "And the only reason he took me out driving was because he needs someone to help out at the pizza shop. You know that." The warm hug Jeff gave me outside the passenger door of his car comes back to me. My stomach flip-flops.

"Julie, Julie!" Paloma and Angie come running into the kitchen. "Piper peed his pants!"

Paloma adds, "Angie was holding him prisoner in the dungeon and wouldn't let him out!"

"Shut up, Paloma!"

Julie's face pales. "On Mom's good couch?"

Soon she's stripping the cover off the soiled cushions and trying to sponge them clean in the laundry room. She tells Angie to help Piper get cleaned up, but Piper rebels. "Don't touch me Angie, you're my *mean* sister. My monster sister! Monster! Monster!"

So Angie helps Julie, instead, and it's me who finds Piper some clean pants and underwear. He picks his Superman underwear, and I tie a blanket around his neck for a cape. I'm singing the Superman theme song when Paloma comes running into the room. "It's burning, it's burning!"

A charred smell is wafting down the hall. I follow the smell to the kitchen and pull open the oven door. The top of the banana loaf is golden brown; it must be burning on the bottom. I yank open drawers and cupboards, searching for oven mitts. No luck. I grab the dish towel and lift the loaf out one-handed. I flip it upside down on the cooling rack. Half the loaf stays stuck to the bottom of the pan.

Paloma peers into the pan and scrunches up her nose. "*Now* what are we going to eat?"

Julie emerges from the laundry room with a wrinkled forehead. "I'm going to catch hell for that."

"Hell! Angie, Julie said hell!" Paloma skips from side to side.

Piper charges into the room, blanket-cape flying behind him, and slams into my legs. I grab the counter to steady myself. "It's not really your fault."

"Oh yes it is, according to them." Her eyes fall on the mangled loaf of banana bread. "What a day."

Julie decides to use the one allotted hour of screen time and plunks the kids down in front of cartoons. The couch is missing one of its cushions. I sit on the floor and lean my back against the base of it. The coffee table stands at desk-height in front of me.

"Do you want to do homework?" I ask.

"Sure," she says. "Just let me go to the bathroom."

I pull our math homework out of my backpack. Julie comes back carrying nail polish, an emery board, and cotton balls.

I raise my eyebrows and turn up my palms.

"Don't freak out," Julie says. "I need to chillax. What is this unit on, anyway?"

"Trigonometry." I read the definition of the word out of the book. "The study of triangles, dealing especially with the relationships between the triangle's sides and angles." I glance up at Julie. She's bent over her nails. I can't tell if she's thinking what I'm thinking: about *love* triangles. About the relationships between Jeff, Julie, and me.

Angie eyes the beauty tools. "I want to do my nails, too. Please?!"

"What would the teachers do if they saw you with painted nails, Angie?"

Angie shrugs. "They wouldn't care."

"They would so." Julie sits cross-legged on the unpeed-on half of the couch. "When I was your age, they used to make me kneel in front of the crucifix and say Hail Mary's for an hour if I came to school wearing nail polish."

"They did not!"

"Did too!"

There's no way I can concentrate on homework, and, besides, I'm getting hungry. It never feels right to raid the Gonzagas' fridge. "I better get going."

"Can't you stay 'til my parents get home?" Julie says.

"It's my turn to make dinner."

Julie snorts. "Like that's much of a job when there's only two people."

"It still takes some time." I stuff my books back into my pack. "Anyway, I've got homework. I'll see you tomorrow, okay?"

The kids have turned their attention back to the TV. Their eyes have glazed over and their jaws hang slack. Julie walks me to the door. "Let me know what happens with Jeff, okay? Don't make me find out from Stacy again."

I don't see why I have to report my every move to Julie. It's not like she's going out with Jeff. But when she touches my arm and fixes on me with her dark-brown eyes, she looks kind of desperate. Like she's begging me. I don't have the heart to refuse. "Okay."

I shoulder my backpack and head for the end of the cul-de-sac. I'm about to start down the footpath that cuts to the next road when I swivel to look back at Julie's house. She's still standing in the doorway, watching me, one hand on the inside door knob. It looks like she wants to switch places with me. To escape from her life.

Until now, I never thought I had anything Julie would want. She's the one who has everything: the looks, the bod. A job she's good at. A real family with sisters and a brother. Parents who are still together. Dudes who want to date her.

But as I wave to her and turn to go, it hits me: I've got freedom. My Learner's. And maybe someday even . . . Jeff.

6

ACCIDENT

It's lab day in Chem. It's hard to know where to sit in that class. Half the class wants to be doctors, and the other half keeps trying to make crystal meth during our labs. A couple of guys singed off their eyebrows last week with the flame from a Bunsen burner. Unlucky for me, I have to wait in line for the bathroom between classes and then haul ass from one end of the school to the other. The only stool left when I get to Chem is at their table.

"Aren't you the one who hangs out with Jeff Minh?" the shorter one says.

The gossip mill at this school is unreal. Why

should anyone care if Jeff and I go for coffee at Timmys, anyway? Or does he just mean hang out in the casual sense, as in, Jeff's in my group of friends? Either way, I ignore the question. "Aren't you the dudes who had an accident in class last week?"

The taller one wiggles the place where his eyebrows used to be. "That's us."

The guys with no eyebrows aren't allowed to operate the equipment because of their accident, so the teacher, Mr. Jones, comes up to our table. "This is a chance for all of you to stretch yourselves. Mary, you've proven that you have excellent powers of observation. You write clear and detailed reports. But this time, instead of observing, you'll perform the experiment. Scott and Todd, instead of doing it, you'll watch and record. How does that role reversal sound to all of you?"

Just delightful. Thank you very much. As if these jokers will ever write anything down. They're just going to stand around and make fun of me, and I'll have to do all the work.

I put on the safety goggles.

"Nice shades!" Scott says. He's the taller one.

"Nice eyebrows," I say.

"Touché." He strokes his eyebrow stubble with the tips of his fingers. "But I'm growing them out, you know." He lisps in a high voice. "They're at that awkward in-between stage."

The teacher calls this an experiment in alchemy. We're supposed to change copper to silver and then to gold. He's given each team some old pennies he keeps in a jar under the demonstration table. I weigh sodium chloride and add it to vinegar in a beaker.

I drop the dirty copper coins into the beaker and stir. Pretty soon they're shining like new. With the tongs, I lift each penny out, rinse it with water, and dry it on a towel.

"Your turn, guys. You have to record the weight of each of these pennies."

I drop the first one onto the scale.

"How do you read this thing?" Scott says.

"It's right here — see?" I point to the numbers.

"Let's just write that down for all of them," Todd says. "They're obviously going to weigh the same. They're pennies!"

"Fine." I sigh. "Just do it, okay?"

I measure zinc and sodium hydroxide into an evaporating dish. The instructions say to heat up the dish, preferably on a hot plate. I check our work space. We don't have a hot plate. I go get Mr. Jones.

The teacher eyes the three of us and then scans the room. Everyone else is in mid-experiment, using their hot plates. He stands lost in thought.

I clear my throat. "Mr. Jones. What do you want us to do?"

He frowns. "There is one other option."

Why do teachers drag things out when they could just give you a straight answer? "Yeah?"

"You can use a Bunsen burner with a ring support."

Scott and Todd look at each other and laugh.

"But Mary is the only one allowed to touch the equipment. Got that, guys?"

"No problemo," they say in unison.

Mr. Jones brings the Bunsen burner out from under his demonstration table and sets it up at our station. I place the dish on the ring support. I turn on the gas and light it with a match. I pull my hand away fast and twist the tube to make a low, blue flame underneath the dish. It lulls me to watch the flame burning steadily.

The solution bubbles. Sure enough, the pennies turn silver. I get excited in spite of myself. "Look at this, guys!"

The solution bubbles faster. Scott bends down close to the dish. The solution has come to a boil, and it spatters Scott's face. He yells and knocks over the Bunsen burner. The dish shatters, and the acid spills over the counter. On its side, the Bunsen burner keeps hissing. The flame shoots out like a blow torch, setting my notebook on fire.

Footsteps thump behind me. "Stand back!" a voice booms. I'm shoved out of the way. Mr. Jones douses the fire with an extinguisher and turns the gas off. He takes Scott by the elbow and leads him to the sink.

"My face, man, my face!"

Mr. Jones bends Scott at the hips, kind of like he's a G.I. Joe. He turns on the tap and rinses the side of Scott's face. The water runs on and on. All the other students abandon their experiments to gawk. Todd keeps asking, "Should I pull the fire alarm? Mr. Jones, should I pull the fire alarm?"

"We've got it under control now, thank you, Todd."

Scott stands up, holding a cloth to his face. One eye squints shut. Mr. Jones holds Scott around the shoulders and faces the class. "Scott's face was splattered with sodium hydroxide. This happened because his team allowed the solution to come to an active boil." Mr. Jones fixes my eyes with his. "Which the instructions said, in bold, capital letters, not to do."

I drop my eyes to the charred pages of my notebook and wonder who I can get the notes from.

"If the solution had splashed Scott's eye,

we would be taking him straight to the hospital. As it is, Scott's partners will stay after class and clean up the lab."

Scott says he'd like to go to the hospital, just as a precaution, and he can find his own way there. I glare at him. He probably didn't get splashed at all. It's just an excuse to skip school.

But Mr. Jones writes him a note and lets him go. As for Todd and me, he orders us around for close to an hour, long after everyone else has finished their experiments and gone home. I salvage our silver pennies from the floor. I rinse and dry them and put them in my pocket.

Mr. Jones finally dismisses us. In the hallway, Todd says, "Thanks for getting me a detention." His voice crackles with sarcasm.

My mouth falls open. "What?!"

"Guess you owe us one, me and Scott, that is. I mean, you put him in the hospital."

I'm exhausted from cleaning the lab, but Todd riles me up. "I never told Scott to stick his face into the beaker! You both should have read the directions. Take some responsibility!"

Todd shifts his feet and looks past my shoulder down the hall. I turn my head to see what he's looking at, but there's nothing there. Just squares of linoleum flooring that stretch all the way to the side exit of the building. On a bulletin board beside us, the grade nines have pinned up posters on lab safety. A disintegrating hand in a bucket of fluid, a skull and crossbones, a flame that looks like a pine tree. I snap my head back, and Todd locks eyes with me. "So, you and Jeff . . . How close are you two?" His tone of voice has totally changed. It's softer, like he's trying to convince me to trust him. "Come on, you can tell me. It's cool."

This is crazy. Nobody knows I have a crush on Jeff, not even Julie. Clutching my books against my chest, I spin to face the other direction and run down the empty hall.

Todd calls after me. "Rice chaser!"

My cheeks burn and my eyes fill with tears. I lunge out the door and take off in a run.

7

RIDE-ALONG

"A ride-along?"

"Yeah," Jeff says. "I've got to come out your way to make a delivery, anyway. So I'll pick you up, show you what to do. Like when you did job shadowing for Socials."

"Job shadowing was a joke. I still can't believe I let Julie talk me into shadowing a cosmetician at London Drugs with her."

"Makeup wasn't your thing, huh?" He chuckles. "Now's your chance to try something else. Come on, you know you're into driving."

Holding the phone, I turn and look out my

bedroom window. I need a job so that I can buy a car. I'm just not sure I want *this* job. For one thing, Jeff's pizza shop delivers until the wee hours to some pretty sketchy addresses. It's probably not the best job for a scrawny sixteen-year-old girl who barely scrapes five feet.

For another thing, Mom would kill me. The whole probationary licence thing. But she won't be home 'til midnight, and it can't hurt to find out more. Besides, it's a chance to spend Friday night with Jeff Minh. *Who am I kidding?*

"I'm in."

***

The smell of pizza hits me when I open the door to Jeff's car. "Hop in!" he says. "First stop is right around the corner."

"So, how many deliveries do you make in one trip?" I spent some time thinking up questions before he picked me up, so I wouldn't be so tongue-tied this time.

"Three boxes will fit in the warming bag. We try to make sure we've got at least one full bag before we make a run. It's not worth it, otherwise."

Jeff heads down into Grandview. He pulls up in front of a small one-storey house.

"First thing I do is double-check the address and make sure they're getting the right pizza." He unzips the warming bag and slides out the top box. A handwritten receipt is stuck to the front of it. He glances at it. "Make sure to zip the bag back up, so the other pizzas stay warm." He opens the driverside door and steps out of the car. Then he ducks back down to put his head in the door. "What are you waiting for?"

I unbuckle my seat belt and follow him up a cement path to the house. A hedge brushes the railing of the front steps and lines the walls under the windows.

A grey-haired lady answers the door. Deep wrinkles criss-cross her face, but her eyes twinkle. "You've come for dinner! And you've brought a friend! How lovely." I half expect her to reach up and pinch Jeff's cheeks. "Will you both stay and share a slice with me tonight?"

She smiles with perfectly even teeth — dentures, I guess — and her smile is contagious. I find myself grinning back at her.

"Mrs. MacKenzie, you know we'd love to," Jeff says, "but then all of our other customers would go hungry."

"Such a thoughtful boy." She winks at me. "You hang onto him — he's a keeper!"

I bow my head and glance at Jeff out of the corners of my eyes, but he doesn't seem embarrassed by the lady's comment. Without looking at the receipt, she hands Jeff some folded-up bills. "Keep the change, love."

Jeff jogs back down the path. "Got to keep up the pace!" When we're back in the car, he says, "Mrs. MacKenzie's a regular."

"I thought so. You ever stay for a slice?"

"I did once, at the end of the run on a slow night. She's been a steady customer ever since."

Jeff takes 50th Street across Coronation Park, and then turns left into Parkvale. The next house we pull up in front of is tall and thin. The wooden steps are sagging, and some junk is strewn around the yard. In an upper-storey window hangs an Edmonton Oilers flag. Someone flips it up and peeks out, then quickly drops it shut. Jeff takes the remaining two pizzas from the bag.

"Hey, what about checking the address?"

"Good call! But these guys are regulars, too, and the last two boxes are both for them. Otherwise, I'd check. Coming?"

A big guy with a soul patch and curly hair opens the door. He's wearing a black T-shirt that says *UFC* in lime-green letters. He looks about twenty-five. A couple of other dudes crowd in behind him, jostling to be first at the food. Jeff has to hang on tight to the boxes. Once the UFC fan pays, the other two disappear with the pizza.

"Hey, this is Mer — Mary," Jeff says. "She might be your delivery girl soon."

The customer sizes me up. "What is she, twelve?"

"Sixteen," I snap.

He opens his mouth in a jackhammer laugh. "Still barely legal." He leers.

I turn and run down the steps. I'm already buckled in when Jeff catches up with me. "Sorry 'bout that. You've got to ignore idiots when you're working. Part of the job."

I shudder to shake off the leftover creepy feeling. Jeff pulls into the road. As he drives downtown, he keeps checking his rear-view mirror. He pulls into the alley behind the shop. "So? What did you think? Easy?"

"I liked the old lady."

Jeff grins. "Mrs. Mac's sweet, and she tips well. But we get most of our business from these monster houses full of guys. Rig workers with big appetites."

"And no cooking skills."

"You got it. Welcome to Phat Pizza."

A vehicle pulls into the other end of the alley. In outline, it looks like an SUV. Its lights shine in on us. They flash on and off, twice, then stay dark.

"Wait here."

Jeff slips out of the car holding the warming bag. He strolls down the alley, swinging it. The SUV's front passenger door opens, but no one gets out. Jeff steps in close and grabs the top edge of the open door. The door hides most of his body. He stands there for a minute, then steps back. Someone pulls the passenger door shut. Jeff pats the roof of the vehicle, then lopes back to me.

"Hey, Meringue. You good for another run?"

Midnight is still a ways off. "As long as you can drop me back home at the end of it."

"Done." He disappears into the back door of the restaurant. After he's gone, the lights come up in the car at the end of the alley. They shine in on me. I shrink down in the seat, so my head barely clears the dashboard. It's uncomfortable to be seen without knowing who's looking at you. The alley is so narrow that I'm expecting the car to back up, but it slowly inches forward.

It draws up alongside Jeff's car with only a few inches to spare. When the side windows are level with each other, the car stops. The driver looks in at me. At first he's stony-faced, then he flashes a smile. He looks like he could be a cousin of Jeff's, but he's no one I've ever met. He mouths something behind the glass, but I don't feel like rolling down the window to hear him repeat it. The SUV rolls forward. It scrapes the trunk of Jeff's car as it passes. The driver honks and then turns onto the road.

The door of the restaurant swings open and light pours out. Jeff jogs down the small set of stairs, yanks open the back door of the car, and sets three full warming bags onto the back seat.

"That's a lot of pizza."

"Business picks up around this time of night."

We're on the road again, heading north. As we cross the Red Deer River on the 49th Avenue Bridge, I ask, "Who were those guys?"

Jeff doesn't miss a beat. "Suppliers from

Edmonton. They bring specialty items I can't get at the market. We've been featuring some gourmet specials lately, if you hadn't noticed. Like Malabar spinach and garlic."

"So, what did they bring you?"

"Hm?" Jeff is checking the rear-view. "Oh, spices, this time. Makes all the difference. Got to pay attention to detail in this business."

On this run, we go farther into the outskirts of the city, from Glendale north of the river to Lonsdale in the southeast. On a residential street in Eastview, Jeff shifts into park. "Your turn!"

"My turn what?"

"To drive, silly."

"Are you sure? It's after dark!"

"Just for practice. We'll stick to well-lit streets."

"And they better be dead quiet!"

Jeff directs me and gives me little reminders along the way. Signal to turn, look both ways, check the rear-view. At the next address, I stay in the car, and Jeff runs in to make the delivery.

It's a relief when he shows up at the driver-side door. I climb over the stick shift and back into the passenger seat.

We've almost reached my house when he says, "When can you take the test?"

"In two weeks, if I get enough practice in." Then I feel stupid. *Does it sound like I'm angling for a "date"?* "But you know, Jeff, I'm not sure I'm the best person for the job. For one thing, my mom probably won't even let me."

His forehead puckers as he glances at me. Then he rubs a hand over his face. "You're not going to go all Catholic on me, are you?"

"Huh?"

"You know, like Julie. 'My parents won't let me do that' . . .?"

That gets to me. Mom isn't the only reason that I'm hesitating. The truth is, the job scares me. But Jeff's not going to find that out. Not if I can help it. "No," I say. "Of course not."

"Attagirl. Two weeks it is. I'll hunt you down!" He reaches over and squeezes my thigh. A thrill travels up my leg and into my core.

8

JULIE'S NEWS

The next time Steve's over visiting Mom, I ask him if he'll take me out driving. His shaggy eyebrows lift, and he blinks his eyes a few times, fast, as if he's scared. I can see what he's thinking: *Is this kid trying to turn me into her stepdad, already?* But he recovers enough to say, "Sure." And over the next two weeks, he takes me out lots of times. We start at Red Deer College and work our way up to the streets of my neighbourhood and, finally, to Gaetz Avenue. After we drive to Inglewood and back one Sunday, Steve says, "I do believe you're ready for the test, partner."

Which is a good thing, since it's booked for after school the next day.

That morning, I find Julie in the bathroom between classes, drawing a circle around her mouth with lip liner. She's wearing stiletto heel boots and a new dress. Over the past couple of weeks, I've been so obsessed with driving that I haven't been in touch with her much.

Her reflection in the mirror looks innocent enough. The neck of her dress doesn't plunge. It hangs in loose folds. But from behind, the cut-out back shows a lot of skin. I'll bet my lunch money that dress didn't come from the store where she works. Everything about it says "designer boutique."

"What's up, Julie?" I peek into her open purse and whistle. It holds a whole new set of high-end products, everything from foundation to eye shadow to blush. Probably three hundred dollars' worth. "Did your rich auntie die?"

She grins at me. The dark line around her mouth makes her look like a clown. She hasn't filled in the middle. "Guess again, Meringue." Julie pulls the cap off a brand-new lipstick and paints her mouth a rust colour that brings out the bloom in her cheeks. She rubs her lips together.

"You're selling your body?"

She sticks out her tongue at me. "It's kind of big news. Why don't we have lunch, and I'll tell you."

I pull a tube of lip balm out of my pocket.

Julie grabs my free wrist. "Wait. I got you something." She lifts a lipstick out of her makeup bag. It's the same brand that she's using, worth twenty bucks, at least. "It's a special kind for dry lips. Better than Chap-Stick and way more pretty."

I pop off the cap and try it.

"That shade of pink looks really good with your skin."

When I check it out in the mirror, I can see she's right. But something tells me this gift has strings attached. "What's the catch?"

"You know that essay that's due tomorrow

in English?" Julie makes a fish mouth to bring out her cheek bones and raises a brush to her face.

It's not the first time Julie has tried to con me into doing her homework, but usually she plays the pity card. With all her responsibilities at home — cooking, dishes, and babysitting Piper, Paloma, and Angie — sometimes she can't get to her homework 'til late at night, and then she falls asleep at her desk. As an only child, I feel pretty guilty when she lays it on me like that.

But this is the first time she has tried to bribe me. "I don't think so." I slip the lipstick back into her bag.

She pouts, which is hard to do when you're making a fish mouth. I can't help laughing. She perks up and leans into me. "I don't see what the big deal is!" she says. "You could whip that thing off in under an hour. I'll have to spend all night on it." She squeezes my forearm. "Please?" She begs me with her big brown eyes.

"Let's meet for lunch at the food court. You can tell me your news. Then maybe after I can *help* you with your essay."

She wrinkles her nose at me. "Okay."

*****

By the time I reach the food court, Julie is already sipping a caramel latte. Her legs are bare under her dress. She must be freezing. But she doesn't look cold. She's beaming. "Have a seat." She pushes a second latte toward me. "I got you a drink!"

The line snakes from the counter to the door, and I'm glad I don't have to stand in it. I slide into the chair across from her. "What do I owe you?"

Her glossy lips stretch into a smile. "Nothing. It's my treat."

The last time we were at the food court, she didn't even offer me a fry. She's used to guarding her stuff from her younger siblings, so I don't hold it against her. But this is a change. "Wow! Thanks, Jules."

Crowds of people mill around the food court. Surrounded by the wall of white noise, we're in a private bubble.

"So," I say. "What's up?"

One of her knees is bouncing up and down. She keeps shifting like she can't sit still. Something looks different about her eyes. It must be that expensive new makeup.

"Are you ready?" She balls up her fists and holds them to her heart. "I got together with Jeff!" she squeals. She's smiling so wide, the gums are showing above her teeth and her cheeks are bulging out. She claps her hands together under her chin. "Can you believe it?"

It's lucky I'm sitting down. It's like I've been punched in the solar plexus. I feel winded. The roar of the crowd is making me dizzy. My head reels like I'm going to faint. "No, I can't believe it!" I slurp on my latte. *Should I say I need air and make a break for it?*

"I know! I'm so happy. He's so hot!" The words tumble out of her mouth really fast.

"He sure is."

"I think he's going to be the one."

"The one?" *She's planning the wedding already?!*

She grips the table and leans forward, gazing at me. "The one I lose my virginity to." It's not just high-end mascara that's making her eyes look different. Her pupils have expanded. They're huge. *Are the infatuation hormones doing that to her?*

I have to make up an excuse. "Shit, Julie, I just remembered. I have a test next period in French. I'm going to have to go back and cram."

Julie frowns. "Really? I thought we were going to hang out and catch up, maybe do a little shopping." She sniffs and wipes the back of her hand under her nose.

I stand up, feeling shaky. "That'd be great, but I have to take a rain check. I'm really sorry." *Shopping: that reminds me.* "I thought your news had something to do with your new clothes and makeup."

"It does." Julie closes her eyes and places

her hand just below her throat. "It was all a gift from Jeff. He took me shopping in Edmonton on Sunday." She lists the stores they visited one by one, so fast I can barely keep track.

I hang onto the back of the chair and take a few breaths.

"Isn't he amazing?" she says.

It's amazing, alright, considering Jeff's supposedly saving money for dental school. "Well, congratulations again, Julie. You . . . you deserve it."

I plow through the crowd to the door and make it to the sidewalk. Sobs are building in my lungs. *Stupid, stupid, stupid.* I was going to surprise Jeff by telling him I had my licence. He doesn't even know I've been practising with Steve. I was avoiding even talking to Jeff because I didn't want to spoil the surprise. *Stupid, stupid, stupid.*

Afternoon classes pass in a blur. At the end of the day, I'm heading home on auto pilot when a horn honks behind me. Someone yells, "Mary!" and I spin around.

Steve is leaning out the window of his black pickup truck. His plaid-flannelled elbow is hooked on the side of the car. I forgot. He offered to leave work early and drive me to the licensing office for my test. I drag myself over to his truck and climb in. A coffee mug pokes out of the cup holder, along with empty wrappers from Burger King. "You look like someone just ran over your dog," he says.

"I don't have a dog."

"Not anymore, you don't." Steve squints at me. "You going to be alright?"

I turn my head away from him and lean my forehead on the window. Tears are pooling in my eyes, and my nose is running.

"Where's your mom when we need her, eh?" Steve blows out air. "Listen. You want to go through with this test or not? It's no good taking a test if you're . . . distracted. You could, well, you could fail, and that would make things worse." I keep sobbing into the window. "I know what I'm talking about, 'cause I had to take the driver's test three times. Once you fail, it's really hard to get your guts up again. Then you freeze up and make the same damn mistakes." He clears his throat. "Like I said, it took me three times. Better not do that if you can help it."

I wipe my eyes and nose on my sleeve. "Okay."

"Okay what?" Steve sounds surprised. I think he'd given up on getting a response from me.

"I'll put off the test."

"Great. Maybe I should make a call." On his cell, he calls directory, gets put through to the licensing office, and cancels my test. "We have to pay the fee, anyway? But that's not right. My niece here has a bad stomach flu. You want her puking in the middle of the test? Because she will, she'll go right down there and puke on the examiner if you want her to, won't you, honey?" Steve winks at me. "Well. We're just trying to keep that from happening."

Steve's white lie makes me smile, and for a

minute the pain lifts out of my chest. When he ends the call, he says, "I got off an hour early and now I've got nowhere to go. Want to get ice cream?"

At Dairy Queen, I order a hot fudge sundae. Between licks of his soft-serve vanilla cone, Steve makes me laugh a couple more times. He doesn't pry into why I was crying. It's a relief.

He dabs his mouth with a napkin. "Hey, I found something out that might cheer you up a bit."

"Yeah?"

"I was looking into licensing for the scooter, just in case I ever needed to ride it."

"And?"

"Your mom's scooter counts as a moped, so you're fully legal to ride it with just your Learner's."

"You're kidding."

"It's the truth, I swear. Just make sure you're off the road an hour after the sun goes down."

It's not the same as a car, but it's something. "Thanks. That's good to know."

When Stacy comes in, I almost don't recognize her without her Tim Hortons uniform. It's when she darts her eyes back and forth between me and Steve that I know it's her. I roll my eyes at her. *Get a life, chick.*

9

DONNY

When the weekend comes, I don't even bother calling Julie. I'm planted in front of the TV watching reality shows when Mom walks in. "Mind if I join you?"

"Go ahead." Eyes on the screen, I grab a cushion and prop it against my side. It forms a low wall between Mom and me.

"I'm sorry about the driver's test," she says.

"I'll take it another time. It's no big deal."

"Steve said you were pretty upset." She pauses. "You want to talk about it?"

"Nope."

She looks past me through the window at

the street. Steve will be here soon to pick her up. "I thought maybe it had to do with Jeff."

A tight feeling grips my stomach, and I snap my head toward her. "What do you mean?"

"You said he offered you a job." Her voice is gentle. "I thought maybe it fell through, and you were disappointed."

I slump back against the couch. She's partly right. I can't work for Jeff, but not because the job fell through. Because I skipped the driver's test. He doesn't want me on cash or in the kitchen. He needs me on deliveries. But she's not supposed to know that.

She touches my shoulder. "I know how much you want to earn money and be independent. I just want to say, I think it's great."

I yank the pillow over my belly and hold it there. It sucks to hide stuff when she's trying to be understanding.

Luckily, Steve pulls up just then. She gives me a kiss on the forehead and says she'll be back by midnight.

***

During a commercial, I reach my hands into my pockets and find a couple of coins. When I rub them together, they feel strange. I pull them out and then I remember: they're the silver pennies from Chem class. The alchemy experiment had one more step. Mr. Jones's voice echoes in my head: "This time, don't watch. Do."

I find a pair of scissors to use as tongs and pinch one silver penny between the blades. I flick on my lighter and heat the coin. In a few seconds, it changes colour. I heat it for three more seconds and then I douse it in a glass of water. I dry and polish it on my shirt tail, then uncover it: a gold coin.

It's fake, of course. I changed the colour, not the weight. Real gold weighs a lot more. There's something the coin reminds me of. That's right, a saying: *All that glitters is not gold.* I wonder what it's supposed to mean. Julie sure likes glittery things, and she doesn't go for the cheap stuff, either.

The ringing of the phone startles me.

Julie says, "Hey, what are you doing to-night?"

"Not much. What's up?"

Background noise clogs her end of the line. It sounds like she's at a party or on a busy sidewalk. "There's an emergency, Meringue, and we're wondering if you can help."

"Who's we?"

"Me and Jeff."

My heart flutters. "What's going on?"

"Jeff's car broke down, and he needs help with deliveries."

I give a snort. "How am I supposed to help with that?"

"We're wondering . . . can you borrow your mom's scooter?"

They have a lot of nerve to ask me! Then again, I never told either of them about my crush on Jeff. No wonder they're clueless about how I'm feeling. Jeff's still my friend. Even if he *is* dating Julie. Out the window, there's still a lot of light in the sky. *Screw it.*

"Yeah. I can do that."

"Awesome."

Before she can hang up, I say, "But I have to be off the road an hour after the sun goes down. And I don't want to do deliveries alone."

"Don't worry. I'll come with you."

I pull on Mom's white riding jacket, along with the pants, gloves, and helmet, then look at myself in the mirror: I'm totally disguised in her astronaut suit. No one can tell it's me. No one can tell I'm sixteen. I snag the keys from the nail beside the door. In the carport, I push up the kickstand with my toe and mount the bike. I keep one foot on the ground. It's been a while since I rode it, but it's not that different from riding a bike, and I've been doing that for years. I turn the key in the ignition, squeeze the brake, and press the start button.

I turn the handle and the scooter surges forward. I tuck both feet up on the deck. Easing up on the gas, I roll down the driveway.

A neighbour two units over waves at me. She must think I'm Mom. I fan my fingers without letting go of the handlebar.

I take side streets until I get downtown. There's a parking spot just big enough for a scooter right in front of Phat Pizza.

Julie runs out. "Drive around to the alley in back. I'll meet you there."

It always feels like something shady is going down in the alley: the dim light, the garbage bins, the urine smell. Julie appears in the back doorway carrying two warming bags. She teeters down the steps with them. She shows me the list of addresses: North Red Deer, then Parkvale.

"Shit, Julie! I forgot to bring a helmet for you!"

Julie's mouth drops open and she flicks her gaze back and forth from me to the scooter. "Can you go alone?"

"How could I even carry the bags? They're too big to fit under the seat."

Julie takes a deep breath and glances over

her shoulder at the back door to the restaurant. "Then let's just risk it."

She climbs on, holding the warming bags in front of her. She pushes up against me and pinches the bags between us by clasping her arms around my waist.

"Do your parents know where you are tonight, Julie?"

"Nah. My cousin's covering for me."

I pull into traffic and circle the block once, to get the hang of doubling again. At any moment, we could get pulled over for Julie's missing helmet. But at least we're in this together. It feels good to be helping out, even if Jeff is dating Julie. He didn't really break my heart; he just scratched it. *Where is he, anyway?*

I steer us onto a one-way street that heads straight out of downtown. Pretty soon we're crossing the 49th Avenue Bridge to the north side of town. Julie shouts directions. After a few wrong turns, we end up in a rundown neighbourhood. The houses are old and close together. The yards are full of junk or over-grown weeds. We pass a house that looks cared for, with fresh paint and cut grass. But the side of the garden shed has been tagged with spray paint.

Julie taps me on the back, and I pull over. She hops off the scooter, unzips one of the bags, and pulls out a box. "Wait here. I'll just be a sec."

I have to turn sideways in my seat to hang onto the warming bags. She hurries to the front door. It opens right away. All I can see of the person who answers is a silhouette. The door closes again within less than a minute, and Julie runs back to me.

"Let's go!"

I rev the engine and pull back into the street. We're done with the north side for now, so we head back downtown. She directs me south and then east into Parkvale. As we get closer, I recognize the address. It's the narrow, three-storey house with the Edmonton Oilers flag for a curtain, where the guy called me "barely legal."

Music is thumping inside the house. A monster truck fills the driveway. This time when the door opens, an arm reaches out and pulls Julie inside. The door slams shut.

Five minutes go by. I'm seriously thinking of going in after her, but I don't have a way to lock up the scooter. I can take the key with me, but that doesn't seem like enough. The stress is getting to me, and I can't think of a solution.

Finally, Julie emerges from the house and speed walks to me. She climbs on behind me, and I twist to face her. "What happened in there?"

She opens her mouth to say something, but her jaw just hangs there. Her eyelids pull back and her face freezes.

"What is it? Julie?"

"You ladies realize you need a helmet for the passenger, as well as the driver, don't you?"

The RCMP car is right beside us, the window rolled down.

"Yes, sir, officer!" Julie's voice has climbed half an octave. "Thanks for the reminder! I left mine inside. Meringue, come and help me find it."

The cop looks like he's on the verge of asking more questions, so I yank the key from the ignition and follow Julie.

She turns the handle of the front door to let herself in, but it's locked. She knocks and rings frantically. On the street, the cops are still watching us. The sun hangs low in the sky.

"Let's run around to the back," I say.

"No. Act casual! It's not a crime to forget your helmet."

"But what are we going to do? You don't have one! They're going to wait until we come back out."

"No, they're not."

"Then they'll come in here after us."

"Not without a warrant."

The door finally opens. "Hey, baby girl!" It's the big guy with the soul patch and curly hair I met before. His black T-shirt says

Make 'em Bite. "Back so soon? You want to do another —"

Julie pushes in past him and pulls me after her. The dude looks beyond us to the street and whistles. "The Mounties. Good call to come back inside. And who's your friend?" I'm glad he doesn't remember me.

"Mary," Julie says. She hasn't called me that in months.

"Tex. Take off your helmet and stay awhile, Mary."

Staying is the last thing I want to do. I've got to get home at sundown. But I don't see what choice I have. The house smells of mildew and cigarettes.

Tex leans down and says something to Julie. Her laugh sounds hard and bright. She puts her hand on his arm and struts beside him like a runway model. *Why is she acting so chummy with this dude?* It's not like her to be so bold with a stranger. I tag behind. Gangster rap blares from the stereo. A couple of couches full of people take up most of the living room. The men, all in jeans and T-shirts, look to be in their twenties or even older. Tucked between the men are two women in mini-skirts. Three boxes of pizza lie open on the coffee table. On the big-screen TV in the corner, a hockey game is playing.

Tex takes a seat in a La-Z-Boy and pats the arm. Julie perches beside him.

"Hey, everyone! The Queen's cowboys just paid a visit, so Julie and her friend Mary here are going to hang with us for a bit."

"Wicked," says one of the guys without a woman beside him. "Let's do tequila shots."

"That's a frickin' awesome idea," Tex says. "Julie, be a doll and bring us some lime from the kitchen, okay?"

Julie looks startled to be put on kitchen duty, but she recovers and flashes him a smile. "Of course."

I follow her into the kitchen.

"Meringue, take off your helmet, you look ridiculous!"

I flip up the visor instead. "I look ridiculous?

What about you? Private cocktail waitress to rig pigs?"

"You better watch what you say, Meringue. These are Jeff's customers." Julie opens the fridge and squats to look in the bottom drawer. She palms a couple of limes and straightens up. "But, God, this kitchen is a mess!" She opens one drawer after another. "Finally!" She pulls out a paring knife, examines it, and sticks out her tongue. "Ech!" She scrubs it in the sink and shakes it dry.

Every muscle in my body is firing. Something feels really wrong. I need to get out of this party house. I'm dying to bolt out the kitchen door, the one that leads to outside. I feel like a sprinter waiting for the starting gun. My right knee jiggles. *How can Julie just stand there slicing limes?* It's like she's numb.

The doorbell rings. Julie freezes. The music goes quiet. Rustling sounds come from the living room, and one of the dudes darts into the kitchen and out the back door. Floor boards squeak as someone walks to the front of the house. The front door opens, and Tex's voice booms. "Bro! What's happening?"

The music gets cranked back up, and Julie blasts into motion. She's slicing so fast I'm afraid she's going to cut herself. Every so often she sniffs and wipes her nose on the back of her hand.

"Have you got a cold?"

"Huh?" Julie looks up from the cutting board.

"You keep sniffing."

"Oh! Allergies."

"Since when do you have allergies?"

"Since . . . I don't know! What's it to you? Maybe I'm allergic to this house, or these limes, or your perfume."

"I'm not wearing perfume."

"Hello, ladies." A deep voice booms from the entrance to the kitchen. I twist toward it. The owner of the voice towers over me. He's wider than three of me. He must have had his black leather jacket custom-made. He has a beak-shaped nose and a buzz cut that makes him nearly bald. He turns toward Julie. He pulls a hand out of the pocket of his dress pants and extends it. "I'm Donny. And you are?"

Julie flicks her eyes up at him. She takes his hand and giggles like she's meeting a rock star. "Julie."

The giant dude lifts her hand to his mouth and kisses it. A scaly curl of red ink climbs out from under his shirt collar. The tattoo crawls up his neck and toward his ear.

"I like your studs," Julie says. "Are those real diamonds?"

Trust Julie to notice the jewellery. He doesn't answer, but he gives her a close-lipped smile that seems to mean "of course."

He turns to me. His eyes are set deep in his puffy, white face. There's no way I'm shaking his hand. I inch a little closer to the door. He smirks. "You must be Julie's BFF."

I look at the floor. "Meringue."

He doesn't sound it out or ask me to re-peat it the way almost everyone does. "Nice helmet, Meringue." He slips his hand back into his pocket. "Safety first."

Julie giggles. "Are you doing tequila shots tonight, Donny?" She sounds like a waitress angling for tips.

The big man shakes his head. "Thanks, but I'm not staying. Just making sure my friends have everything they need tonight." Donny swivels his head back and forth from me to Julie. "Do you two realize you're exactly the same height? I bet you're always getting asked to model. It's hard to find petite ladies who are built so perfectly."

I back up against a wall and cross my arms in front of my chest. "How long are you planning to stay here, Julie?"

"'Til the coast is clear." She's placing the lime wedges onto a plate.

I meet Julie's gaze and raise my eyebrows in a plea.

Donny's watching us. "Is there something I can help you ladies with?"

"No," I say.

Julie shrugs. "Meringue didn't bring a helmet for me, and the cops just stopped us. She wants to go home, but I need a ride back down to Phat Pizza."

Like a cat that glimpses a wounded bird, Donny zeroes in on Julie. His eyes drill into her. "Phat Pizza? You're the delivery girl?"

We answer at the same time. "No," I say.

"Yeah," Julie says. "Just for tonight." She tilts her head at me. "We're helping out a friend."

"And who's that?"

He's too nosy, and he's a stranger. There's no reason to tell him stuff. "No one special," I say.

"Jeff Minh," Julie says.

"Julie!" I glare at her.

Donny swings to face me. "And you're the driver." A grin spreads across his face.

Tex bursts into the kitchen. "The shooters are ready when you are, ladies."

Julie hands him the plate. "So are the limes."

Donny says, "But we've got to split."

Tex's face falls. "Really? Can't you stay for one shot?"

Donny throws his arm around Julie's shoulder. "This little lady is coming with me."

I suck in my breath, but Julie giggles and nuzzles into Donny like she's known him for years.

Tex takes a step back and raises his hands in the air like someone pulled a gun on him. "Sorry man. No disrespect, hey?"

"Looks like you have enough pizza to keep you going all night, huh, Tex?"

Tex's eyes flicker with worry. "My bro made the call without asking me, I swear. Sorry man. We're tapped out."

Donny mumbles something I can't hear. He holds up his hand like he's inviting Tex to an arm wrestle. Instead, they clap palms, and Tex's face relaxes.

Donny and Julie have their backs to me. The door's within reach now. I grab the knob, twist it, and pull. The night air smells fresh. I slip out and pull the door shut behind me.

I run down the porch stairs and around the house. The scooter is waiting for me on the side of the road. The cop car has disappeared. On the horizon, the sunset glows orange.

10

BAGGIE

Julie and I have a spare together, and we're heading to the mall to grab coffee. I haven't seen her since the weekend. When I got home on Saturday night, I kept texting her to make sure Donny — that beak-nosed, walrus-sized guy — got her back to Phat Pizza safely. She didn't reply until the next day. I hardly slept that night.

"Do you think you can get your mom's scooter again?" she says.

"Why? Didn't Jeff get his car fixed?"

"Hm?"

"Jeff. Car. Fixed?"

"Oh. Yeah." At an intersection, she sways on the curb, not looking at me.

"What was wrong with it?"

"Beats me. I don't understand cars. You'll have to ask him."

Inside the mall, Julie takes the long way around to the food court. She probably wants to show off her outfit. She's sporting a new pair of designer jeans and a cowl-necked sweater. The salesgirls hover near the entrances to the shops, sizing us up as we pass by.

Julie fingers a blouse on a sales rack in front of a store and makes a face. "Polyester."

A lot of my clothes are polyester. As if she didn't know. An edge slips into my voice. "What do you prefer?"

Julie purses her lips. "Bamboo, or some-times silk."

I grab her by the elbow and pull her along. There's a sick feeling in the pit of my stom-ach. Julie works one shift a week, and her parents make her put some of her earnings into a savings account. "How are you paying for this stuff?"

She pushes me away. "You think I'm stealing or something?"

When she's mad, she's more likely to blurt stuff out, so I bug her. "Remember those three hours we spent locked in the basement of the mall last year? Getting interrogated? The detectives are probably still trailing us to this day."

She kicks a cement garbage container. "That was so unfair! I swear I *forgot* to take those earrings out."

A security guard strolls past in the opposite aisle. He watches us with a poker face. The Muzak isn't loud enough to drown us out.

Julie lowers her voice. "God. I'm not shoplifting."

Feet come pounding behind us. Someone bumps into Julie and knocks her purse to the floor. It spills open, and her stuff scatters everywhere. The guy keeps running. Julie falls to her knees and grabs her makeup. About a foot away, something plastic catches my eye. It's a tiny bag, the size that might hold a pair of earrings or contact lenses. Just as the security guard shows up, I cover it with my foot.

"Are you alright?" he asks Julie. "Did he take anything?"

Julie shakes her head and bursts into tears.

The security guard narrows his eyes as she scoops the new cosmetics into her purse. "Do you have a receipt for those items, miss?"

While his back is turned toward me, I squat down and slip the thing out from under my shoe. I stand up and shove it deep into my jeans pocket. Julie blubbers to the guard that she bought the stuff in Edmonton last week. She opens a lipstick and says, "See? It's smudged. Those are my lip prints. They're from this morning. Or here." She flips up the lid of a makeup compact. "I used this yesterday. See how the sponge is coloured with makeup, but dry? That proves it. It's been used, but I didn't just use it. So, I couldn't have stolen it from your mall, now could I?"

I can almost picture Julie in a courtroom making a case about the evidence. Meanwhile, the security guard actually blushes. It's like Julie has just shown him the stains on her underwear. He lets us go.

On the way back to school, Julie rummages in her purse, swearing non-stop. I push my hand into my jeans pocket and curl my fingers around the baggie. For a minute, I thought it might be artificial sweetener. I don't think that anymore.

"Lose something, Julie?"

She glares at me. "Leave me alone."

So, I do.

***

After school, even though Mom isn't home, I shut the door to my room and push my dresser against it. I pull out the baggie from my jeans. It's about the size of a restaurant packet of salt or pepper. But it's made of clear plastic and has a zip-lock on one end. It holds white granules, so fine they're almost powdery. There's also a strip of paper inside, like the fortune from a fortune cookie. I flip the bag over. Typed on the paper is a phone number: 771-987-0445. Nothing else.

I boot up my computer and run some image searches. After a few clicks, I'm pretty sure what I found in Julie's purse is not leather preservative, or kosher salt, or sucralose.

It's cocaine.

My fingers still hover over the keyboard, but my arms are shaking. *Where did she get it? And what is she doing with it?*

I get up and pace back and forth in my room. Window to door.

Door to window.

Window to door.

I read the number again. I don't recognize it, but it's printed in Julie's favourite font. I can picture her cutting up the strip of paper and stuffing it into the baggie.

There are two things I need to do: one, tell

Julie I'm on to her. And two, get rid of the drugs before Mom comes home.

To scare some sense into Julie, I dial *67 to block my number. Then I call the number from the strip of paper.

Ring. Ring. Click. "Yeah."

It's not Julie. It's not Jeff. It's a man with a deep, scratchy voice. My heart thumps harder. My throat dries up, and when I speak, my voice breaks. "Sorry, I think I've got the wrong number."

There's a pause. "You sure?"

My mind races. *Maybe I can milk him for information.* I'll pretend to be a customer. Like an undercover detective. "No." I swallow. "Actually, I got this number from a friend."

"Go on."

"And, I was wondering, if I wanted to get the same thing she got, how would I . . ."

"You'd need forty bucks."

"Uh-huh."

"You got the money, kid?"

My palms are slick with sweat. "Um."

"I don't like people wasting my time."

The tone of his voice makes me shudder. I don't say anything.

"Why don't you call back when you've got the money. Then we'll talk."

"Okay."

He hangs up on me.

The phone slips out of my hand. My knees buckle, and I sink to the floor. My heart is still pounding. I have no idea who I just talked to, but he was no high-school kid. Even though I blocked the call, it feels creepy that I talked to him in my bedroom. *What was Julie doing with his number?*

Donny. Beak-nosed, walrus-sized Donny. Is he a coke dealer?

I'm about to call Julie's cell when I glance at the clock: 4:30 p.m. Mom will be home soon.

Time to tackle Problem No. 2: Getting Rid of the Drugs.

Flushing them down the toilet would be

easy. I push the dresser clear of my bedroom door. In the bathroom, I lift the toilet lid and look down at the bowl. A grungy brown line is forming at the high water mark. *Gross*. Mom leaves this bathroom for me to take care of. It's obviously time to clean.

I'm stalling.

The thing is, Julie might try to deny everything. If I flush down the drugs, I won't have any proof. If I keep them, I can show her, and she'll have to fess up.

The toilet lid shuts with a clack.

Maybe I can bury the baggie somewhere. But not in the yard. Our neighbour's dog digs up anything we plant. I don't see why cocaine would be an exception.

My head feels like it's being pinched. Figuring out where to hide cocaine is not my usual after-school dilemma. I just have to get out of here. Walking makes it easier to think.

With the baggie tucked into my front pocket, I pull on my hoodie and shove my feet into my shoes. As I head down the road, I watch for ditches or garden beds that might make a good burial site. The road is lined with cement sidewalks and strips of grass. A vacant lot looks promising, but a lady is letting her dog run around in it. No point in stopping. Loitering would look suspicious.

I walk 'til I'm out of my neighbourhood. Everyone who passes can see what I'm trying to do. At least, that's how it feels. I keep my eyes on the ground.

Someone says, "Hey, Meringue."

I look up to see a couple of smokers in front of a coffee shop. It's the guys from Chem. I've avoided them since the day of our accident. Their eyebrows have grown back in. I look at the taller one, Scott. "How's your face?"

He grazes his cheek with his fingertips. "It's fine. Wasn't a big deal."

"What do you mean?" the shorter one says. "She put you in the hospital!"

The two guys look at each other. They seem to be having a conversation without saying a word. Todd, the shorter one, darts his eyes, and Scott shakes his head. People pass by and jostle me. It's getting to be rush hour, and my errand is nagging at me. *Maybe I can bury the stuff at the playground on the corner?*

Todd punches Scott on the shoulder. "Ask her!"

I flick my eyes back and forth from one to the other. "Ask me what?"

Scott straightens up. "Are you in business with JJ?"

"Who?"

"Jeff and Julie." Todd spits it out.

I do a double-take. Jeff and Julie are my two closest friends in Red Deer, but I didn't know people were calling them "JJ." Or "in business." "No." I look at the ground and shuffle my feet.

I expect them to sneer and ditch me. But when I raise my head, their eyes are still on me. It dawns on me that they don't believe me. Something makes me add, "Not really."

"But kind of?" Todd says.

"Why do you want to know?"

"Forget it," Scott says.

But Todd speaks up. He flings his arms wide. "We're bored, what do you think?" He looks up and down the sidewalk and lowers his voice. "We want to do some lines."

It's almost like they know I have drugs to get rid of. I can't shake the feeling that everyone can see through me.

I move down the sidewalk, leaving the coffee shop behind.

They keep up with me. Todd isn't much taller than me. He gives me a silly grin. "Don't worry, we won't tell."

I cover a block and then another, with the two dudes right at my heels.

We're at the park on the corner. There's no chance of burying anything with these two trailing my every move.

"Are we going to have to follow you all the way home? Is that where you keep your stash?" Todd isn't smiling anymore. "Good to know."

The threat of being followed home makes

me panic. I've got to get rid of these guys.
There's only one way I can think of to make
them leave me alone. *What the hell.* I reach
into my jeans and pass the baggie to Todd. I
glimpse the phone number on the white piece
of paper just as he snatches the bag from my
hand. He pockets it right away. All that the
passersby see are three teenagers chatting by
the monkey bars.

Scott says, "What do you want for that?"

My face stiffens. I wasn't trying to sell it.

Todd says, "We've each got a twenty."

They pull crumpled bills out of their pockets and stretch out their hands. I raise my
palm underneath theirs, they wipe the money across it, and I clench my fist. It's done. I
walk away.

11

STASH

Three days later, my phone rings as I'm arriving at school. When I see Julie's number on the screen, my stomach flips. She hasn't even texted for three days. *Has she figured out that I took the baggie? Did Scott and Todd tell?* I answer the call and wait for her to yell at me. But she sounds happy. She's skipping school and treating herself to a spa day. She tells me to meet her at the hair salon at lunch.

All morning, I psych myself up to tell her everything. The crumpled twenties are still stuffed in my jeans pocket.

Her appointment isn't finished when I

arrive — surprise, surprise — so I take a seat and leaf through fashion magazines.

I look over when I hear her ring tone. It's coming from her purse, which is on the floor beside her chair. I meet her eyes in the mirror. She raises her eyebrows and nods at the phone. I walk over to her.

Julie's hairdresser whirls around her, picking up tools and then switching them for others like a magician pulling tricks from a hat. I'm not about to interrupt his pro routine by handing Julie the phone. I pull it from her purse and head for the waiting area. Julie pouts at me in the mirror until her hairdresser teases her about having a secretary. Then she laughs.

"Hello?"

"Julie." It's a deep, scratchy voice. "We haven't met yet, but I work with Donny. I saw you at the bar the other night."

When was Julie at a bar? I can't think of anything to say, but the man doesn't seem to notice.

"Donny needs to know, Jules. Did you bring Jeff on board?" It's the same voice that answered when I called the number from the baggie. I'm almost sure of it.

Julie looks trapped in that salon chair. The cape hides her whole body. Only her head and hands show, like a cartoon character in the stocks.

"It's a yes or no question, Julie."

"I know."

His voice booms. "Don't you remember the deal you made with Donny?"

I find my lighter in my jeans pocket and rub my thumb over the end of it. At times like this, having something to fidget with really helps. "Can you remind me?"

"All those Long Island Iced Teas went to your head the other night, huh."

I force a giggle. "Uh-huh." *Maybe that's why she wasn't answering my texts last Saturday night.* She was at a bar getting drunk with Donny.

"The deal was, you bring Jeff on board or

else you show us his stash. You have until midnight."

He hangs up. I press a key to check the number of the last incoming call. 771-987-0445. I'm not especially good with numbers, but I've seen that area code only once before: on the strip of paper in the baggie.

I pocket the phone. While the hairdresser styles and blow-dries Julie's hair, my mind reels. *Jeff has his own drug stash?* I can't believe it. He's always been a straight-A student. The future dentist.

Julie struts to the counter, and the hairdresser helps her into her coat. He gently pulls her long hair out from under the collar and drapes it over her shoulders. I've never seen her look so pretty. Or so grown up.

We leave the salon and go window shopping. She keeps flicking her hair over her shoulders. She's using a shoe store window as a mirror to check herself out when she remembers the phone call. "Who was it?"

"Beats me, but Donny needs to know if you brought Jeff on board."

She whirls to face me with wide eyes. She sticks out her hand. "Give me my phone back."

I pull it from my pocket. She snatches it, pushes a button, looks at the screen, and sighs. "What else did he say?"

"He said you have 'til midnight to bring Jeff on board, or else you have to show him Jeff's stash."

Julie's jaw drops open and her pupils dilate 'til her eyes look black. "I'm so fucked."

"Julie, what's going on? Who are these guys?"

She bites her lip and shakes her head. "Never mind."

"But Jules!" I need to tell her about the mall, the baggie, the phone number, the guys from Chem . . . It's all happening so fast.

She's crying. I put my hand on her shoulder, and she flicks it off like I'm a drunk guy groping her. Then she stands still and looks me in the eyes. A memory flashes into my mind of the first time she really looked at me. I'd been following her around at school for days, trying to get her attention. One day she finally noticed me. She sized me up like I was a homeless puppy. I could tell she felt sorry for me, but she also knew I could cause her some trouble. She had to weigh both sides. Finally, she made a decision. "It's okay. You can sit with us."

Today, the same look crosses her face. She's deciding whether or not to tell me what's going on. She's deciding whether to trust me. "You better not tell *anyone* what you just heard. I never meant for you to answer the phone! I just wanted you to pass it to me. You just had to butt in, didn't you?"

Julie stalks down the street so fast she turns an ankle and her shoe falls off. I catch up with her. "Are you okay?"

She squats to pick up her shoe. Tears streak her face, and her nose is running. "Does it look like I'm okay?"

I can't stand to see her like this. "Julie, let me help. We can go to the police."

She straightens up. Her lips quiver. In her high heels, she towers over me. "Don't you dare. Don't you ever . . . I should never have let you . . .!" She growls and takes off down the sidewalk.

I run after her and grab her arm. She seizes my wrist and flings it away from her. "Meringue. Stay away from me. I mean it. And if you care about me at all —"

"I do! I'd do anything to help —"

"Then keep your mouth shut. Don't say a word to anyone. Just forget what you heard."

She hurries to the end of the block. She rounds the corner toward downtown and disappears without looking back.

12

SHACK

Mom sprays on her Happy perfume and buttons up her favourite blouse. Must be date night. She asks if I want to join her and Steve for a movie. "We're going to the plaza," Mom says. "You say your friends wouldn't be caught dead there. So there's no danger of being seen with us."

"Thanks, but I'd rather stay in."

She lifts her eyebrows in surprise. I've got to make it more convincing.

"I already downloaded a movie, and Julie might come by."

Mom slides in close to me and squeezes my

shoulders. "Will you be alright if I stay over at Steve's tonight?"

"No problem. I'll be fine."

She looks relieved. She shrugs into her space suit and adjusts her helmet. I have to admit, she looks pretty cool pulling out of the driveway on her red machine. Her lemony smell lingers in the air after she leaves.

I flop onto the couch and cross my ankles on the coffee table. I try Julie's cell. No answer. I pull a pack of paper matches out of my pocket and tear one off. I can hear Julie mocking me. "Making another match person?" But I don't care. It soothes me.

I press redial. No answer.

I split the stem of the match into arms and legs. I bend each limb where an elbow or a knee would be. I fold the tips to make hands and feet. I'm working on getting the feet just right so that the little guy stands up. He teeters and falls a few times before he finally balances.

Julie's tear-streaked face floats into my

mind. She might really be in danger. *How can I help if she won't take my calls?* She said, "Don't say a word to anyone." But Jeff doesn't count. He's already involved. He's the only one I can turn to.

He answers after two rings. "What's up, Meringue?"

"Do you know Donny?"

"Who?" Rap music is playing in the background. It doesn't sound like he's at the restaurant.

"That big guy. The one who drove Julie back to the shop the other night after we got busted in Parkvale."

The music dies. Jeff must have gone through a door. He hisses, "You got *busted*?"

"For not having a helmet."

Jeff exhales. "Right. What about him?"

"I'm worried about Julie. I think she's with him tonight."

"What do you mean?"

I blurt it out. "She's going to show him your stash at midnight."

Jeff curses. "Don't say anything else." He pauses. "I'll pick you up in fifteen."

While I watch for Jeff, I set my match person inside the metal windowsill. I strike a fresh match and touch it to him. His head explodes with a sulphur smell. The trunk of his body gets charred, but the flame dies out before it reaches the ends of his arms and legs.

Headlights sweep the drive. A horn honks, and I run outside and climb into the front passenger seat. Jeff's wearing his black leather jacket. He's gelled his hair so that the ends spike a little. A hands-free cell is clipped to his ear. Its green casing shines like a June bug. He guns the engine as we pull away. "How much has Julie told you?"

Not much, but he doesn't need to know that. "You're dealing coke."

Jeff snorts. "Probably told you that after doing lines. She has a habit of blabbing too much, but when she's on blow, it's even worse."

"Blow?"

He glances at me. "Cocaine."

My mouth falls open. My core temperature seems to plummet, and I shudder.

"Haven't you noticed her acting like a diva and talking a mile a minute?"

I don't want to believe that Julie is using. But my stomach knots up. It could be true. She was so bold with those men at the party house.

"Watch for huge pupils and random sniffing, too," he says.

Check. Check.

He shakes his head and clicks his tongue. "Dead giveaways."

Crap. My best friend's a cokehead?!

"What else did she tell you?" Jeff asks.

I flesh out the story about the phone call, and Julie's deal with Donny. "She was supposed to bring you 'on board' or else show them your stash."

Jeff reaches into the inside pocket of his jacket and pulls out a cigarette. I've hardly ever seen him smoke. He lights up and takes a long drag. He doesn't seem like the same guy who coached me on driving a few weeks ago.

I make my voice as casual as I can. "How did you get into this?"

He doesn't reply. He just keeps smoking. His face looks tough.

"I mean, I'm not sure this is going to look so good on your application for dental school."

A pained expression flashes over his face. It's just a glimmer, but it gives me hope that the old Jeff is still there, under the surface.

"You can tell me," I say. "I won't judge."

"If you really want to know —"

"Yeah?"

"— a couple of months ago, these other Vietnamese guys came up to me when I was leaving work. They were looking for someone with the last name Minh. They told me stuff. By the time we all figured out that I wasn't the guy they were looking for, it was kind of too late. I knew too much. They said I had to help them out."

I cough from the smoke and roll down my window. "Help them out?"

"Yeah." He sounds kind of ashamed. "With deliveries." He brings the cigarette to his mouth again.

"Is that why you needed help at the shop? You wanted me to take over delivering pizza, so you could deliver . . . coke?"

He glances at me and takes a breath as if he's going to say something more. Then he closes his mouth and nods.

We drive on in silence. I drum my fingers on the armrest. Questions race through my mind, but I settle on one. "How does Donny fit in?"

"Hell if I know. I've never even met him. All Julie said was that he gave her a ride that night. Sounds like there was a lot more to it."

Outside the window, city lights dwindle and dark fields open up. He exits the highway and makes one turn after another until we're on a narrow country lane, a Township Road. He slows down as we approach a clump of trees. He drives off the road onto the dirt, circles around the trees, and parks behind them.

"You should stay with the car," he says.

"No!" My stomach flutters. "I don't want to stay by myself."

He groans. "Okay, come with me, then. But don't make a sound."

From the road, I turn back to look for the car. It's fully screened by the trees and the darkness. Jeff crosses the road and jumps a ditch. I stay on his heels. We pick our way through overgrown bushes. An old wooden fence snags my pant leg as I climb over it. An open field stretches before us. Thank God for the full moon tonight because every couple of feet we hit another cow pie. *Cow pie*. Pretty stupid name for a big pile of crap, if you ask me.

We tromp across the field until a building comes into view. I don't think it's big enough for a barn. It might be called a shack, or a shed. It looks pretty run down. The shingles are crooked, and the roof sags in the middle.

Some of the windows are broken and sealed from the inside with black paper. It gives me the creeps. The skin on my arms breaks out in goose pimples. I don't want to get any closer.

Jeff peels ahead and disappears around the side of the building. I inch forward behind him. When I'm nearly at the shed, he comes back. He doesn't seem to be carrying anything, but his coat is zipped up and it's bulging a bit.

A deep voice sounds. Jeff freezes. He grabs my hand and drags me the few feet to the shed. A pile of lumber lies beside it. Jeff dives between the lumber pile and the shed. The voice rumbles again, and I lower myself down. A loose nail scrapes my calf, and I suck in my breath. Jeff turns onto his right side, and I tuck myself in behind him.

My heart is thumping. I breathe through my mouth because it's quieter. The wooden door to the shed opens, and heavy steps pound the floor. Bangs and thuds and curses trickle out.

I strain my ears. "Did you give it to him?"

The words are muffled a bit, but it sounds like Donny.

"He doesn't want to join." It's Julie's voice.

"I said, did you give it to him?"

"Yes."

Slap. Julie cries out. Beside me, Jeff's body jerks.

"Don't lie to me, bitch."

Julie whimpers. The man takes a few heavy steps that shake the building to its foundation. The next time he speaks, his voice is louder. He must be right on the other side of the wall. "Billy here says he got a call from a couple of kids who go to your school. They got the number from the freebie. They say a chick sold it to them for forty bucks."

"It wasn't me!"

My body trembles all over. *The freebie.* The baggie that spilled out of her purse that day at the mall. It was *me* who sold it.

"Thing is, the freebie wasn't meant for re-sale." Donny has slowed down his speech. Each word drops like a stone from his mouth.

"You sell it, you're working for us."

I can't make out what Julie says, but from the tone of her voice, she's pleading with him. They move away from the wall.

Then it goes quiet. Somebody moves around inside the shed. Wooden planks groan and squeak as they're forced to give under pressure. After a while, a third voice chimes in, low and gruff. The door scrapes open.

"Hang on a sec, sweetheart. Unless you want to watch us." Donny's voice comes from the end of the shed. The other male voice chuckles beside him.

The beam from a flashlight shoots past the end of the shed and lights up the grass. If they take two more steps, they'll round the corner. They'll see us. Jeff takes shallow breaths. My heart almost explodes in my chest.

The sound is like water coming from a hose and hitting the side of a house. It reminds me of Mom watering the garden. A wave of homesickness rocks me. I could be safe in my bed. Instead, I'm listening to a pair of drug lords take a piss.

"Fuck, man, this fucking cow shit. Why would anyone set up out here?"

"'Cause they're hicks, man." It's that deep, scratchy voice, the one from the phone. "What do you expect in a town this size?"

"Right." The sound of a fly zipping up. "You think the bitch told them to move their stash?"

"She must have. I checked all the floorboards, all the walls. Even the rafters. Nothing there. Just the scale and the lamp. Good thing I brought my own rocks. Got to be chopping every spare minute, seems like."

The voices fade as the men move away.

Something rattles, and there's a hissing sound like a gas leak. I picture the shed bursting into flames with Julie inside it.

"Move it, Jules. Party's over."

The shed door scrapes open and shut again. Jeff doesn't move a muscle, and neither do I. There's the faint, fruity smell of his hair gel. My breath is condensing into a wet patch on the shoulder of his coat. I don't know how much time goes by before a car starts in the distance. The sound of the engine streaks south, past the place where Jeff's car is hidden. When it dies out, Jeff rolls onto his stomach, pushes himself to his hands and knees, and then stands up. My right arm has gone to sleep, and it tingles with pins and needles as I struggle to my feet. We crawl to the front of the shack. The door has been tagged with spray paint. It looks like initials: P.A.

Jeff turns and sprints across the field. I follow, but I twist my ankle on a gopher hole and fall. I have to run-hop the rest of the way, ankle throbbing. When I reach the border of trees that divides the field from the road, twigs snap underfoot. I suck in my breath. I'm shaking as I climb the fence and jump the ditch.

Jeff's car isn't there.

It takes me a second to remember that he hid it behind the trees on the other side of the road. I limp to the car and crawl in.

He's holding an unlit cigarette between his

lips. "Have you got a light?"

My fingers feel like they're made of rubber. It takes all my concentration to dig out my plastic lighter and flick it. Jeff leans into the flame and takes a drag, then starts up the car. As he smokes, I rub my thumb over the spark wheel until my skin feels alive again.

"Did you see that tag?" Jeff asks.

The road runs parallel to the field. Jeff follows it north. He's not going back the way we came.

"It looked like initials."

"Yeah. P.A. Do you have any idea what that stands for, Meringue?"

I rack my brain. "Public announcement?"

We reach an intersection. One street sign says *TWP RD* and the other says *RGE RD*. Each one is followed by a number that I can't make out.

"Don't be a dumb ass." His voice is hoarse. "It stands for People's Army. They're a gang! We're talking serious, organized crime. I'm not messing with them."

"What's the difference? I mean, aren't you already . . .?"

Jeff holds the wheel and the cigarette in one hand while he rakes his hair with the other. "Think of it this way, Meringue. The Vietnamese guys I told you about are like a Ma and Pa coffee shop. P.A. is like Starbucks, only with guns. They want to swallow us up or take us down."

He's flooring it toward the highway.

"What are you going to do?"

"I'm sure as hell not joining them!" He rubs the back of his neck. "I need to get out."

"That — stuff — you just picked up . . . can you give it back?"

Jeff shakes his head. "They fronted it to me. They want the money in a week. They're going to drive back down from Edmonton to collect."

"What happens if you just give it back next week, instead of giving them cash?"

"I'm not sure, but I have a pretty good idea." He exhales. The smoke gets sucked out the window. "And it would hurt like hell."

We've reached another intersection. Jeff

turns right. We're heading south on Highway QE2. The only sound is the hum of the engine. The voices from inside the shack echo in my mind. "What about Julie?"

He frowns. "Sounds like she was supposed to recruit me. She never even tried. Maybe she knew it was a waste of breath." He takes another drag. "But then she led P.A. right to our base. I don't get it. Why would she do that?"

"I don't think she *wanted* to! I think she was forced. I mean, Donny slapped her around in there!"

Jeff winces. "I hope she's alright." He grinds out his cigarette in the ashtray. "But I'm not getting sucked into the big leagues, by Julie or anyone else. Like I said, I'm getting out."

"In a week."

"That's right."

He punches the stereo and music blares out. Ahead, the lights of Red Deer loom closer and closer.

13

NOSEBLEED

On Sundays, Julie has a routine. She sleeps 'til noon and then walks a couple of blocks to the café on Morningside for a chocolate croissant and a double latte. Halfway between her place and the café, there's a small park with a playground and bushes. I stake it out. It's one of the first warm days in May. A bunch of kids are playing on the jungle gym while their parents sip coffee from white paper cups. One of the benches is screened by a hedge. I sit down on it to wait.

Julie rounds the corner just after twelve, wearing sunglasses. She drags her heels like she's still half asleep. She looks just the same as always, which makes me so happy that I jump up to approach her. My ankle twinges and slows me down. Before I can get close to Julie, someone else steps out from the other side of the hedge and makes a beeline for her. It's a woman who looks like she might be here at the park with her kids. Middle-aged and wearing a track suit.

Julie smiles and acts like she knows the woman. She hugs her and then pulls back and draws her hands down the woman's arms, like she can't get over how good it is to see her. At the end of the long, slow pull, they clasp hands for a second. Then Julie lets go and walks on. The woman keeps one hand closed in a fist. She hops into a car and drives away. An empty baby carrier is strapped into the back seat.

I shrink back against the hedge, hoping Julie won't look over. Her flip-flops slap against the soles of her feet. After she passes the park, the sound still carries.

I huddle in the shade. It doesn't matter if Julie looks the same on the outside. Inside, she's changed so much it scares me. But I have to talk to her. I force myself to follow her to the café. I'm only limping a little.

She's at the counter placing her order. I get into line behind her. "An iced latte, please."

She turns her head when she hears my voice.

I sift through my wallet for change. "Hi, Julie."

I can't see her expression under the sunglasses. We wait in silence for our drinks. She tears a corner off her pastry and nibbles on it.

"How's the croissant?"

"Same as always."

"That's nice." I scuff my toe on the tile floor. "It's nice when things stay the same."

Julie turns her head away from me and pretends to study the bulletin board. Dog groomers and babysitters for hire. Classes in Zumba and yoga being held.

The barista sets down our drinks at the

same time. I pick mine up and follow Julie outside. She leans against the warm, brown shingles on the side of the building. I join her, and the sun beats down on our chests.

I'm trying to figure out where to begin when she says, "It's over between me and Jeff."

"Really?" I wish she would take off the damn sunglasses and let me see her eyes.

"He won't take my calls." She sniffs and a tear rolls out from under her shades. "He texted me, 'Stop calling. It's over.'"

A man and a woman walk up to the door of the café and pull it open. The bell jingles.

Julie lifts her sunglasses halfway up and wipes her eyes. They're bloodshot with dark circles underneath. "I wish I'd never gotten into this." She sets the shades back down on her nose.

I touch her arm. "Then just get out, Julie."

She shakes her head and sobs. "I can't."

Out of all the questions whirling in my head, I try to pick the most important one. "Are you working for P.A. now?"

She hooks my elbow and leads me away from the café, as fast as her flip-flops will carry her. We're back at the park before she stops. "You shouldn't even know that name."

"Well, I do. Jeff and I were outside the shed last night when you got there. We heard everything! We saw the tag."

Her hand trembles as she takes her coffee back from me. The kids at the playground have migrated to blankets and are munching on crackers. Julie moves shakily over to the swing set. Her knees buckle, and she drops into a swing. "You told Jeff about the phone call you butted in on at the hair salon? Even though I begged you not to say anything!"

I lower myself into the swing beside her. "I was trying to help! I was worried about you. I still am." The chain-link is cold against the palms of my hands.

She won't meet my eye. "Do you know what you've done? They think it was *me* who told Jeff to move the stash. They figure it was worth at least three grand. So, now I have to work for them until I've paid off the money!"

I gasp. "That sucks."

"Ye-ah."

She wouldn't be trapped if it weren't for me. "I'm so sorry." But there's another side. "Of course, Jeff would have been screwed if he hadn't moved it."

Julie drops her chin and whispers, "I know."

We sit there in silence. A crow lands on the cross bar of the swing set and eyes Julie's pastry bag.

I clear my throat. "There's something else."

Julie scowls. "Now what?"

"That day at the mall, when you spilled your purse. I picked something up off the floor."

She flicks up her sunglasses. "What?"

"That . . . baggie."

"*You* took it?" She drops her croissant bag as she jumps to her feet. "Why didn't you tell me? What did you do with it?"

"I got rid of it."

"How?"

"I guess, I, well . . ." My mouth won't let me form the words.

"Did you sell it?"

"At first I was going to bury it because . . . Oh, it was a stupid idea. But then these guys were following me and asking me for it, and finally I just gave in. I let them have it and then they gave me money. So, yeah. I guess I sold it."

Julie is staring at me. "It was *you*. I can't believe you! Donny thinks I sold it and kept the money. He thinks I lied. That's why he hit me last night."

I cringe. "We heard. Are you okay?"

She touches her cheek. "It sounded worse than it was." She shivers. "But I'm scared of them. I'm scared of what they'll do."

A weight presses down on my chest, and I hunch my shoulders. If only I could go back in time. I could have just given the baggie back to Julie when we left the mall. But I was curious! She wasn't telling me anything. And I was feeling so left out. "What were you supposed to do with it, anyway?"

She grabs a chain attached to one of the swings. "Give it to Jeff. Donny wanted to recruit him."

"But why would Jeff want to work for Donny?"

"Donny's stuff is higher-grade than Jeff's. So it costs more. Jeff could make more money." She sighs. "But I knew he wouldn't join. So I didn't think it really mattered when I lost the sample."

I twist in the swing and look up at her. "It didn't matter?! But if Jeff wouldn't join, you had to show them his stash."

Her eyebrows pinch together. "That wasn't part of the original deal! I would have remembered that. I didn't find out about *that* until *you* told me." She shoves the chain and the empty swing jerks back and forth.

"Donny doesn't play fair." A dry laugh escapes from my throat. "You'd almost think he was a gangster or something." The jibe is out of my mouth before I can think better of it.

Julie frowns and crosses her arms in front

of her chest. After a minute, her eyes darken and she gasps. "It all makes sense now! On the drive out, he kept talking about 'changing the rules' and 'getting in the game' like it was me who started it. It's because he thought I went behind his back and sold the freebie. That's why he made me take him to the shed in the first place."

As she pieces the puzzle together, I feel even worse about selling the baggie. The memory of lying on the cold ground listening to Donny's voice makes me shudder. Fear is clouding my thoughts. Then my mind clears for a second. "Julie. Why don't we go to the police?"

"No way. If I snitch, I'm dead."

"You seriously think they'd kill you?"

Her lower lip trembles. "I can't take the chance. Besides . . ." She stares into space. The crow glides to the ground and takes a few bow-legged steps. It hops toward the pastry bag and then away from it, like it's doing the hokey-pokey.

"What?"

She shakes her head. "I've already done too much. So has Jeff. If we went to the police, they'd charge us with trafficking. Our parents would disown us. Our lives would be over!" A frown stretches across her face the way it does when she's about to cry. Sobs catch in her throat.

I'm partly to blame for the trouble she's in. I owe it to her to help. "Will it make a difference if you tell them it was me who sold the freebie? And —" My voice breaks. "It was me who tipped Jeff off? Will it help you get out?" A jolt of fear rips through me. I don't want Donny to be reminded I exist. *If he's trapped Julie into working for him, what's to stop me from being next?*

She shakes her head. "It won't work. He'll just go after you, too." She looks me in the eye. "And there's no way I want you to end up like me."

Relief pours over me, but a guilty feeling lingers in my belly. "There must be something I can do."

"No." She sniffs. "Well, actually, there is."

My heart leaps. "Anything!"

"Have you got a Kleenex?" She gives a strangled laugh.

I check the pocket of my fleece and pull out a tissue. Julie dabs her nose with the Kleenex. It comes away with bright red spots on it.

"I think you've got a nosebleed." I rummage for another Kleenex in my pocket. "Here."

The sight of the bloody tissue makes Julie cry harder. "Look at me! I'm so pathetic. I'm such a mess."

A car rumbles to a halt in front of the playground. It's a black two-door sports car. Rap music blares from the open windows. Julie runs off without saying goodbye. She lets herself into the front passenger seat. As the car curves in a tight U-turn, I throw myself back in the swing. I'm hanging in a flat line, my head level with my toes. This way, if the driver turns his head, he won't see my face. Donny's seen me once, but I don't want to let

him get a second look. I don't want him coming for me.

After the car squeals away, I sit up again.
The blue-black crow rips open the paper bag
with its beak and flies off with Julie's chocolate croissant.

14

DRIVER

I slam on the brakes at the sight of a jogger on the curb. She trots across the zebra stripes in front of Steve's truck. Her legs flash in tight fuchsia leotards. In the corner of my eye, my road test examiner — a man well into his fifties — checks the jogger out.

He catches me looking and clears his throat. "Good braking." He ticks a box on his clipboard. "I'll just get you to parallel park and then we're done."

Luckily, the curb is wide open. I don't have to fit between two other cars, which is when it really gets hard. Steve told me they wouldn't ask me to do that in case I damaged an innocent bystander's car. Guess he knew what he was talking about. I crank the wheel back and forth, shifting from reverse to drive and back again. When I'm done, the examiner cracks open the door. "Two inches from the curb. Perfect!"

At the licensing office, I drive into the turn-around, brake, and shift into park.

"Congratulations!" The examiner holds out his hand for me to shake. "You've earned your Class 5 licence."

On the sidewalk, Steve is trying to catch my eye. I give him a thumbs-up, and he punches his fist toward the sky.

***

Mom can't get off work 'til later, so Steve and I celebrate at Dairy Queen. As he eats his burger across from me in the booth, I stick my spoon into my hot-fudge sundae. "What do you do if your friends get into trouble and you want to help them out?"

Steve doesn't really know who my friends are, so it seems safer to ask him than Mom. "That depends," he says between bites.

"On what?"

Steve finishes chewing and swallows. "The kind of friends and the kind of trouble." He holds up an index finger. "First of all, are they good friends?"

I think about that for a minute. When Jeff and Julie first got into trouble, they didn't drag me into it. I didn't like feeling left out, but it seems like they wanted to protect me. And now Julie's working for Donny to pay for mistakes I made. Only a good friend would do that. "Yes."

He adds his middle finger, so that he's making a peace sign. "Second, is it the kind of trouble you have to get into yourself to help them get out of?"

The cold ice cream hurts my teeth. I swish the tip of my tongue around my mouth to make the sting go away. "I don't know. Maybe."

"Remember what they taught you in swim

class: 'If you see someone in trouble, don't attempt a rescue.' Lots of people drown trying to save someone else."

I set down my spoon. "You're just supposed to let them sink?"

"No." Steve sucks on the straw poking out of his drink. "You're supposed to tell a lifeguard."

I scoop up another spoonful of my sundae.

"Now, in this situation—" With his two peace fingers, Steve gestures back and forth between his own chest and me. "I'm not the lifeguard, am I? Because if I'm the lifeguard—"

A text message arrives. It's Jeff. *How did the test go?*

An electric shock runs through me. I forgot that I told him the date of my test. "I have to use the washroom."

"Sure, go ahead and avoid the question."

"You're not the lifeguard."

When I'm in the washroom, another text arrives. *Got yr licence? Cd REALLY use u tonite.*

Jeff's got only a few days left before his

associates come back down from Edmonton to collect. If he can pay what he owes, he's free. This will all be over.

Julie said there was nothing I could do to help her. But Jeff is asking for my help. He's desperate. I text him back. *Got my Class 5.*

Back at the booth, I ask Steve if he can drop me off at Phat Pizza.

He nods. "Sure. If it's okay with your mom. Just remember: don't attempt a rescue."

***

When I show up at 7:30 p.m., Lee's at the counter. "How's it going?" I ask.

He shrugs. "Pretty busy. Jeff's supposed to be here most of the night, but he's always taking off. It puts all the responsibility on me."

"Sounds tough." I look past his shoulder. "Is he around? He wanted me to work tonight."

Lee's eyebrows shoot up. "Really?"

"Just on deliveries. I got my Class 5 today!"

Jeff breezes into the restaurant from the kitchen. "Meringue — high five!"

We slap our palms together. He's wired, in full-on multi-tasking mode. "Have you got the scooter?"

I pull back in surprise. "No. You didn't ask me to bring it."

"That's cool. You can take my car. Come with me out back."

Jeff puts his hand on my shoulder and steers me through the kitchen and out into the alley. His dark-grey Honda is parked just outside the back door. He lowers his voice. He's pinching my left shoulder with his right hand. "I've got a lot to off-load, Meringue. Stuff's not moving as fast now that there's competition in town. I'm going to hit the nightclubs tonight while you're on the road, okay?"

I hate the idea that I'm making it easier for him to deal drugs. "Is this really the only way out of this?"

"If I don't have the money by the weekend, they'll break my face." He rubs one hand over the back of his neck. "I'm finished by the end of the week. I swear. You can hold me to it."

"I will."

His eyes clear for a moment. He softens his grip on my shoulder, but then takes hold of my other shoulder, too. He bends down and kisses me on the mouth. "You're a lifesaver, kiddo." He releases me. "Just let me load you up."

He disappears into the kitchen. I do an instant replay of the kiss, slowing it down and savouring it. His aim was good: he touched both of his lips to both of mine. Our noses didn't collide. The pressure was firm. There was no slobber. Still, it's not how I imagined a kiss from Jeff. It wasn't tender. It was just a thank-you peck.

He's back with a stack of warming bags and a map. "Forty-five minutes from restaurant to customer is about as long as you want to push it. Otherwise, you get people complaining it tastes like cardboard." He hands me stack of envelopes. "To make things easy, I've got an envelope for each address. Just jot down the address on each one when you get there. The customer will fill the envelope and seal it. That way you're not responsible for counting bills or making change."

"Won't they think that's weird?"

"Not at all. I told everyone it's exact change only." Jeff opens the passenger door and sets the warming bags down on the seat. "It's standard practice when we're training a new delivery person. You've got enough to worry about as it is."

He's right about that. I've got nine pizzas to deliver in forty-five minutes and I've had my licence for exactly four hours. At least the sun is still up. We've got an hour or so before it sets. I check the list of addresses. I'll start north and work my way back down. Mrs. MacKenzie is on the list tonight. It seems safe to leave her 'til the end. She's too nice to complain if the taste is ruined.

The first house is on an upscale street in the Pines. A woman answers the door in a silk bathrobe. Her nightgown is low-cut enough that a rose tattoo shows above her heart. "Sorry if I'm not decent." She pulls the neck of her robe together. "We're staying *in* tonight." She winks at me and laughs. She takes the envelope, stuffs it with cash, and hands it back. "You say hi to Jeff for me."

An address in Glendale is next. They ordered three pizzas, so I'm gearing up for a party house. A jacked-up truck looms in the driveway. It's splattered with mud. On the doorstep, I hold the pizzas in front of me, my arms perpendicular, like a tray. A dude in sweat pants opens the door, scratching his belly. Three days of whiskers darken his jaw. He yells over his shoulder, "Princess Blow is here!" I step back and try to block out his voice. I don't want to know what porn star he's referring to. He takes the envelope from my hand. "You got any brewskis to go with that?"

"Huh?"

Another guy crowds in behind the first one. He has a blond crewcut and an upturned nose.

"You hiding a cooler in the trunk, babe?"

I wish they'd stuff the money in the envelope and be done with it. "No."

"We're kidding!" The first guy punches my shoulder. "Oops, better pay you." He tucks some bills into the envelope.

The blond guy snatches it. "Let me do the honours!" He locks eyes with me, sticks out his tongue, and licks it the length of the envelope. He wiggles his eyebrows like his tongue action is supposed to turn me on. *Gross.* I don't even want to touch the envelope.

At the next few addresses, most of the customers are guys in their twenties or thirties, and most of them get under my skin. A couple of different ones try to make me come inside. One guy actually grabs me, and I have to squirm free. I don't mind doing Jeff a favour this time, but there's no way I want this as a permanent job.

I'm heading to Grandview with my last pizza, for Mrs. MacKenzie, when a red light spins in the rear-view and a siren gives a mini-wail, on and off. *Holy shit*. I'm getting pulled over. I park on the side of the road and roll down my window.

The cop swaggers up to me. "Licence and registration."

I dig out my temporary paper licence and hand it to him. He shines a flashlight on it as I rummage in the glove compartment for the registration.

"Your first day as a probationary driver, huh?"

"Yes." I don't know what's wrong with that. I'm allowed to drive on my own and to be out after dark, according to the rules.

"Congratulations are in order, I guess."

Am I supposed to ask why he pulled me over?

"Where are you headed?"

"Grandview."

"And what are you doing in Grandview?"

"I'm delivering this pizza."

He jots something down in the note-book and then walks back to his car. In the rear-view mirror, I see him talking on his radio. There's a second cop in the passenger seat. Sweat trickles from my armpit down my ribcage. A text arrives from Jeff. I read the screen without opening the message: *W r u?* I've been gone for over an hour. The message light blinks over and over.

Finally the officer lumbers out of his vehicle and drags himself back to my window. "There are a couple of issues."

"Yes?"

"You were driving with only your running lights on. That's why I pulled you over."

"The running lights?"

The officer's expression changes. He looks patient, more like a teacher than a cop. "They come on automatically in most cars. They're for daytime use. But when it actually gets dark, you need headlights."

Damn. Steve's truck had automatic headlights, so I forgot about them.

"That's the first thing." He puts on his cop face again. "The second thing is, you shouldn't be working as a driver until you're through the probationary period. Who are you working for?"

"Actually, I'm not working. I'm just helping out my friend tonight. He's the manager." *I wonder if I can get away with not telling them Jeff's name?*

"And what's your friend's name?"

"Jeff."

"Jeff who?"

"Jeff — I can't remember."

"Is it Jeff Minh? He's the registered owner of this car."

Of course. They already know his name. I nod.

"Chinese fellow, is he?"

"Actually, he's Canadian."

The cop narrows his eyes at me. He sucks his teeth. "Right."

The second cop has appeared out of the shadows. He joins the first one, shoulder to shoulder. "But where is his family from?" He's a younger guy, and his voice is a little bit higher pitched.

"You know, originally? What country?"

"These other Vietnamese guys came up to me," Jeff had said.

In a flash, it's obvious: the cops are on the lookout for those guys and their connections. To protect Jeff, I'm going to have to lie. "I really don't know where his parents came from. We never talk about it. I just know it's somewhere in Asia."

The two men step off a few feet from the car and mutter to each other. Then the older one heads back to me.

"Alright, miss, I'm writing you up with a fine for driving without your headlights on. And your employer is going to get fined for allowing you to work as a driver."

"Okay."

"You can deliver that last pizza, but then I want you off the road, understood?"

"Yes, sir."

He punches some numbers into a hand-held device, and a ticket spits out. He hands it to me. "Now, be safe out there."

"Thank you."

"And Mary —"

I jolt at the sound of my own name. "Yes?"

He grasps the edge of the driverside window, leans down, and looks me in the eye. "You're very young. Choose your friends wisely."

I jerk my head away to break the eye contact. After he leaves, I just hold the steering wheel. The cop car sits behind me for a while. The dome light is on, and every time I glance in the rear-view, the two men are still making notes and chatting. Finally, their headlights come on, and they pull out. As they pass me, the younger one rolls down his window and calls, "Don't forget to turn on your lights!"

***

Mrs. MacKenzie's cottage-style house looks cozy and welcoming when I pull up in front of it. It's at least an hour and a half since I left Phat Pizza. Mrs. Mac smiles gently. "Did you get lost, dear?"

The stress boils over. "Pulled over by the cops and fined!" I break into sobs.

"There, there, come in and have a cup of tea."

"Your pizza is going to taste like leather!"

"Nothing that a zap in the microwave can't fix. Please come in."

I follow her inside to her kitchen. An empty dinner plate sits on her kitchen table. "Have a seat, dear." Mrs. Mac reaches for a second plate from inside her yellow painted cupboards and sets it in front of me. The cuckoo clock ticking on the wall says quarter to ten — it's even later than I thought.

Mrs. Mac opens up the pizza box. "Ham and pineapple! Oops, my order was for Greek. My mouth was watering for that feta cheese."

"I'm so sorry! Please, Mrs. Mac, there's no charge for this. I won't take any money."

"That's okay. I like Hawaiian just as well." She lifts a couple of pieces out with a spatula and slides them on to a paper towel. "What's this? Extra salt? Good heavens, I'm not likely to need that!"

I jump up. A baggie full of white grainy powder lies under the pizza. I pick it up. It's covered in drops of grease.

"How odd!" Mrs. Mac says. "I've never seen them do that before."

"No." I tuck the bag into my pocket. "Me neither. Can I use the bathroom?"

I shut myself into the bathroom and turn on the fan. It whirs and rattles. Good. It'll mask my sobs. The toilet lid is covered in royal blue plush, and I collapse onto it, my chin in my hands. I take deep breaths as what just happened crashes over me.

I've been delivering coke all night. That's what they meant by Princess Blow. My body shakes all over, and Steve's words ring in my ears. "Lots of people drown trying to save someone else. Don't attempt a rescue." *Why didn't I listen to him?*

I stand up and lift the toilet lid. I rip open the plastic and shake the baggie into the toilet.

I flush and the water swirls in the bowl. I wait until all the drugs have been washed away before I lower the lid.

I rinse the plastic bag in the sink and then crumple it up inside some toilet paper. I drop it into the wastebasket.

By the time I make it back to the kitchen, Mrs. Mac is seated at the table and has set a slice of pizza and a cup of tea in each place. I don't have an appetite, but it might calm my nerves for the drive back. My phone rings. Jeff. Instead of answering it, I power off the phone.

I force down a couple of bites. The pizza tastes awful, and I wash it down with tea. Mrs. Mac is too polite to say anything about the taste. She finds out I just got my licence and tells me that she learned to drive at sixty, after her husband died. "Never needed to know how before that. Would you believe it was my daughter who taught me?"

It's hard to focus on what she's saying, but I nod and smile, and hope that my company helps to make up a little bit for being so late and for bringing the wrong pizza. Whoever got her drug-less Greek pizza must be royally pissed, but that's Jeff's problem.

"Drive safely, Mary." Mrs. Mac sees me off at the door.

"I will, Mrs. MacKenzie."

In the alley behind Phat Pizza, I leave the envelopes of money and the car key on the front seat. I knock loud on the back door of the restaurant. Then I take off running.

15

WHITE GIRL

The next day, I leave my phone turned off. I tidy my room, clean the bathroom, do laundry, and help Mom in the garden. Jeff must be pissed at me for screwing up the orders and splitting after only one run, but I'm pissed at him too. He used me.

Mom and I squat to yank weeds. Growing vegetables is her newest craze. She even got Steve to fix the gate so that our neighbour's dog won't dig them up. She says it's healthier and cheaper to grow food than to buy it from the store. I'll believe that when I see it.

She keeps glancing at me, like she wants

to start a conversation. I don't mind rooting around in the dirt, but I'm in no mood to talk. Finally she can't stand the silence anymore. "I'm proud of you for passing your driver's test on the first try," she says. "You're very determined when you want to be."

I try to shut off thoughts of last night. "Steve helped me out a lot."

Mom smiles and her eyes shine. "I'm glad you two get along so well."

"He's alright." I grasp a lacy green leaf. "Is this a weed?"

"No, it's a carrot top. Don't pull it up!"

"It's hard to tell the good plants from the bad ones."

"I know. You have to train your eye." She sits back on her heels and wipes her forehead on her sleeve. "Steve told me you were asking what to do when your friends are in trouble."

I stand up and brush off my hands. "I think we should call Steve 'Sieve.' He sure can't keep anything in."

"Don't be mad at him, honey. He was just

concerned." Mom squints up at me. "Are they really in trouble? I can tell something's on your mind."

It bugs me that she can read me. "It was just something to talk about, Mom."

"Really? Because if you need to talk . . ."

"I don't." I look away. My insides are twisting. I'm mad at Jeff and worried about Julie, but I can't squeal on them. Telling Mom would be the same as going to the police. "I've got to use the bathroom."

***

The land line rings around suppertime.

"Meringue, I've been trying your cell all day!" It's Julie.

"What's up?"

"Jeff's blocked my number. I need your help."

"Yeah?"

"I have to ask him a huge favour."

Mom's within earshot, making lasagna.

"Even though he's not talking to you?" I whisper.

"I've got no choice. Can you bring him out behind Phat Pizza at 8?"

I don't bother explaining that Jeff and I aren't exactly on good terms, either. "I'll see what I can do."

She hangs up. When the receiver starts to honk, I realize I'm still holding it. I press a button and set it down.

Mom says, "Who was it?"

"Julie."

Mom has her back to me as she lays strips of slippery cooked pasta into a baking pan. "You didn't talk for long."

"She had to go." Mom's riding jacket hangs on a peg by the kitchen door. It gives me an idea. "Actually, now that I've got my licence, she wanted to know if I could take her for a spin on the scooter."

"Right now? What about dinner?"

"I'll eat when I get home."

Mom looks over her shoulder at me. "Are

you sure you know what you're doing, Mary?"

"You were the one who taught me to ride it."

She wipes her hands on a dishrag and turns around. "I'm not talking about the scooter." She gives me a searching look.

I shift my feet. "It's okay, Mom. Julie and Jeff were dating and then they broke up, and now they're not talking to each other. Julie's really upset." I stick my hands in my pockets. "It's awkward. I'm kind of caught in the middle."

"Oh." At the mention of dating drama, her face relaxes. "It would be nice of you to take Julie out for a spin, in that case. You're a good friend. But eat something before you go, okay? At least have a trail bar."

"If you insist."

"Don't stay out too late, and please be quiet when you come in." She sighs and rubs the top of her shoulder. "All that gardening did me in. I'll be dead to the world by sunset."

***

At Phat Pizza, I park out front. Lee is bus-sing tables. There's no sign of Julie. Or Jeff. I check my phone. It's quarter to eight. I tuck my helmet under my arm and walk into the shop.

Lee doesn't smile when he sees me. *Has Jeff turned him against me?*

"Hey, what's up?"

Lee grips the edge of the counter. "You didn't hear?"

I shake my head.

"We got broken into last night. The whole kitchen was turned upside-down."

I suck in my breath. "Did they take any-thing?"

"No. The money was in the safe, and other than that, it's just pizza ingredients and pa-per plates. Not much to steal except the oven. Luckily, it doesn't fit through the door."

In all the time I've known Jeff and Lee, they've never mentioned a break-in at the shop. This has got to be because of the drugs.

"Uncle Thuan got the call from the security company last night, and Jeff wasn't even home yet. He had to come down and deal with it himself. He's really mad — he thinks Jeff somehow brought this on. Said it looked like revenge vandalism."

My mouth feels dry. "Really?"

Lee glances behind him. "For one thing, there was spray paint all over the walls and on the back door."

"Did it say anything?"

Lee eyes me as if that's a strange question. "No. Just squiggles. Maybe it would make sense if you're in a gang."

I clear my throat. "Where's Jeff?"

Lee shrugs. "Who knows? Some manager!" He shakes his head. "Uncle Thuan was just grilling me about what's been going on around here, and it's really hard to keep covering for Jeff. Oh, and *your* name came up."

"Huh?"

"Uncle Thuan's being fined because you

delivered pizzas last night. He's totally choked."

A prickly feeling fills my chest. "I'm sorry. I should never have done it."

"It's Jeff's fault more than yours. He's suspended as night manager for now."

I'm not sure what else to say, so when the next customer approaches the counter, I slip away. Outside, I dart around the building and into the alley. The graffiti on the door has already been painted over. I draw close and pull back again, turning my head at different angles to try and read it.

"What the hell happened to you last night?"

I jump and spin around. Jeff's voice has come out in a snarl. It's already shadowy in the alley. Past his shoulder, the stall where his dark-grey Honda is usually parked sits empty. No wonder I didn't hear him arrive. In black running shoes, he steps closer to me. His eyes are bloodshot. "Those guys in Glendale gave me shit — the ones who got Mrs. Mac's Greek pizza."

Anger boils up inside me. "How do you think I felt when I got pulled over by the cops?"

Jeff sneers. "I never thought they'd stop a white girl."

His words hit me. They're hard to absorb. It's like I've swallowed a lump of cement. My breathing gets fast and shallow. *"That's* why you wanted me as a driver. Because I'm white! That's been the reason all along." I scan the ground, my mind racing. "You used me. You said you wanted someone you could trust. You — you — *liar*."

"I didn't lie." Jeff shoves his hands into his pant pockets. "I did trust you." He kicks at something on the ground. "It wasn't *you* who sold me out to P.A."

"You sure as hell didn't tell the whole truth!" *Princess Blow. What country is his family from? They've never given me extra salt before.* The echoes make me tremble. "I didn't know what I was really doing last night. You tricked me! You put me in danger!"

I'm shaking all over as I remember the cops. And the dudes who got the wrong pizza. *What if they'd chased me down?*

"It was just a few nights!" He shuffles his feet.

"A few nights?" The ground seems to be moving underneath me. I can't get a solid footing anywhere. "You mean there was more than one?" My brain searches for memories of delivering pizza. *Bingo.* "The night I 'job shadowed' you."

He groans. "I was hoping you'd never have to know."

There's another one, like a punch to the gut. "The night Julie and I rode the scooter. There was stuff in the pizza, wasn't there? I bet your car didn't even break down that night!" That means Julie tricked me, too — before Donny even came into the picture. "I can't believe you guys didn't tell me."

"It was for your own protection."

I stare at him. "Bullshit. You didn't tell me because you knew I wouldn't do it."

Jeff laughs coldly. "You wouldn't do it, huh?" He shakes his head. "You can drop the Miss Innocent act."

"Huh?"

Jeff looks straight into my eyes. "Todd told me you dealt to him and Scott."

My arms go slack, and my helmet clatters to the ground. My breathing gets shallow again. Jeff and Julie may have tricked me into dealing drugs, but I chose to steal the baggie and sell it to Scott and Todd. That made things worse for Julie. Then Julie made things worse for Jeff. What went around, came around. "We *all* screwed up."

"Yep." Jeff grabs his head, hands clasped behind his neck, and pinches his elbows together. It looks like he's trying to disappear. When he drops his arms, they hang limp by his sides. "But you saved my ass last night, Meringue. If it was me driving, they would have searched the car."

I bend down to pick up my helmet. "Racial profiling?"

"Kind of. I mean, they're tracking these Vietnamese guys. It's a bigger operation than I thought."

"They kept asking me what country your family was from. You're lucky I didn't tell them."

Jeff locks eyes with me. "We're both lucky."

I look back at him, then drop my chin to my chest and nod. Being found with coke would have landed me in trouble, no matter what. "What are you going to do?"

"I hid my car with the rest of the stuff locked in the trunk. I've still got about half of it. But after last night, I can't do business. I'm on the cops' radar. Not to mention my dad's. He's been on the phone all day with family in Edmonton. Everyone's pissed about Vietnamese gangs giving the community a bad name. If he finds out I got involved —" Jeff shudders. "It'll be as bad as getting arrested. Maybe worse."

High heels clip-clop down the sidewalk that

passes the alley. The sound stops. We both jerk our heads to see the silhouette of two people: a massive man and a petite girl. The footsteps start up again as they approach us.

"That you, Minh? I'd like a word."

My whole body trembles when I hear Donny's voice. His hand is clenched around Julie's upper arm. She's moving stiffly, like a hostage, taking two steps for every one of his. She looks so helpless that I can't be mad at her.

"Heard you had a break-in last night." Donny slows down and swaggers on the last few steps. He glances at me. "Still got your underage driver, I see." He points with his chin. "Nice helmet."

He remembers me. Fear roots me to the spot.

Donny turns his attention back to Jeff. "Not too much damage, I hope?"

"You mean you didn't do this yourself?" Jeff tosses his head toward the door. "You sent one of your goons?"

Donny chuckles. "I don't think my men

like that name. Sounds too much like yours."

"Huh?"

"You know. Gook."

Jeff looks like he wants to smash Donny in the face. He clenches his fists and his jaw.

"Of course, you're a little of both, aren't you? A gook goon." Donny's mouth gapes open as he roars.

Jeff cuts him off. "What do you want?"

Donny slings his arm over Julie's shoulders and hugs her to his side. She whimpers. "Your lady friend here is just wondering if you're ready to talk."

For the first time, Jeff looks directly at Julie. A mix of emotions flashes across his face. He looks pained, then angry, then sad.

Donny squeezes Julie. "Go on, kid. Tell him."

Her voice quavers, and she keeps her eyes on the ground. "If you give Donny the rest of your stuff, he'll let me go."

Jeff lunges toward her. "Let you go? What do you mean?"

Julie glances up at Donny. She looks scared.

Donny's voice booms, and Jeff backs up. "Me and this sweet young thing made a little agreement. But she's finding it hard to keep up her end of the deal. I gave her an out, didn't I?" He rubs her shoulder and leers at her. "She didn't like my . . . proposal."

Julie looks like she wants to throw up. So does Jeff.

"So she came up with her own idea. What do you say, Minh?"

Jeff is shifting his weight back and forth, looking like something between a boxer and a tied-up dog. He wrestles with his decision for longer than I expect. Didn't he basically just tell me he was out of options? Finally, he speaks. "Okay."

Julie's eyes light up. She slides out from under Donny's arm. It looks as though she wants to throw herself at Jeff, but she just stands there, teetering on her heels.

Jeff isn't looking at her. "When and where?"

"Burnt Park. Right where the road ends. In two hours."

Julie takes a couple of steps toward me and Jeff, but Donny seizes her elbow.

"Not yet." She winces as he drags her back toward him. "Jeff has to give me something first."

Julie pleads with her eyes, first at Jeff, then at me. Donny snaps her around to face the other direction. They go back the way they came, Julie's neck in the crook of Donny's elbow.

When they disappear out the end of the alley, Jeff curses. He crosses to the recycling bin, pulls out a glass bottle, and hurls it after Donny. It shatters on the pavement. Jeff rests his hands on his hips and sighs.

We just stand there for a while. Finally, I break the silence. "At least he's going to take the stuff off your hands."

Jeff snorts. "Generous, isn't he?"

"Seriously, in two hours, it's over."

He grimaces. "Not for me." He pulls out his phone and checks the time. "Besides, I've got to help Lee in there, and my car's about an hour's walk from here." He bites his lip. "Plus, now I've got to sweep up broken glass."

"I can help."

"Yeah?" He sounds bored. "You're going to sweep?"

"No. It wasn't me who threw the bottle. But I've got a spare helmet. I can double you to your car."

Jeff raises his eyes. "You'd do that? After . . . everything?"

"I'm still mad about it." I place my hand in the middle of his chest and give him a shove. His feet skid backward. "But I helped make this mess. So, I'm going to help you clean it up."

16

BURNT PARK

To kill time, I bus tables. Lee stays on cash, and Jeff keeps the supply of fresh, hot pizza coming from the kitchen. He also answers the phone and spends a lot of time telling customers that there are no deliveries tonight. When the callers stay on the line, Jeff's tone gets less friendly. "No, man, I can't help you . . . Not anymore. Find someone else."

Ninety minutes later, Jeff pulls Lee aside and says something in a low voice. Both of them glance over at me, so I join them.

"Whatever, dude," Lee is saying. "It's not like you're ever here, anyway."

"I promise you, things are going to change."

Lee won't look at him.

Jeff claps me on the shoulder. "Ready to go?"

Outside, we strap on the helmets. "Can I drive?" Jeff says.

"Have you ridden a scooter before?"

"Lots of times."

It beats having to turn my head and listen for directions while trying to steer. Jeff's the one who knows where his car is. "Okay."

I straddle the seat behind him and hug his waist. The smell of his jacket reminds me of the night we were lying side by side next to the shed, hiding from Donny. Tonight, the evening air whips past us, but with my body pressed against Jeff's, I don't get too cold. I close my eyes. It's a relief to let him navigate.

When Jeff slows down, I open my eyes. We're in a new subdivision that hasn't been paved yet. We pass a few houses under construction and keep going to where the lots lie vacant. At the end of a gravel road sits Jeff's car. It's not hidden, exactly, but it's definitely off the beaten path.

Jeff shuts off the engine. I slide off first, and he follows. He holds out the handlebars. "Here."

I grab them. He undoes his helmet, lifts it off, and passes it to me. I have to prop up the kickstand before I can take it.

"Thanks for the ride," he says.

"No problem." I stow the helmet in my backpack and zip it up.

"See you later, eh?" He's bouncing on the balls of his feet, ready to spring. He expects me to leave.

I sling the backpack over my shoulders. "I need to follow you back out of the subdivision."

He twitches and sighs, then glances at the trunk of his car.

"Sorry, I wasn't paying attention," I say. "I don't know where I am. I'll just follow you 'til we get back on a main road."

The sun is sinking, and there are no street lights out here yet.

Jeff clenches his jaw and then marches to the trunk. He opens it, leans in, and moves his hands around inside it.

I follow him. He's opened up a black garbage bag and is unrolling layers of packaging to reveal several plastic zip-lock bags full of white powder. He pulls one out and palms it, feeling its weight.

"What are you doing?"

He glares at me. "Never mind."

"Keeping some for yourself?" I lean in and stare at him. "Are you insane?"

"Why shouldn't I? I'm probably going to get bumped off by my suppliers any day now! Might as well stay numb while I wait." He sets down the bag. "Damn it. I have to take a leak."

Jeff darts to the front of the car. While his back is to me, I sweep up the whole bag of cocaine, run to the scooter, lift the seat, and drop the package into the hold. Then I jump on the seat, start the engine, and take off. Gravel spins under my wheels.

"Hey!" Jeff yells.

I won't be able to outstrip him. I don't really know where to go, anyway. But I couldn't just stand there. It's bad enough that Julie's using. I'm not about to watch Jeff go down the same path.

Jeff's car revs. Pretty soon he pulls level to me with the window rolled down. "Okay, Meringue, you win! Pull over and give it back."

"No! Just lead the way. I'm coming with you."

Jeff throws up his hands and then grabs the steering wheel. He pulls ahead of me, and I tail him as we wind our way out of the suburb and back onto main roads. I keep hoping we won't end up on the QE2, because the scooter only goes seventy kilometres an hour. We'd draw attention to ourselves for sure, and maybe get pulled over. My armpits are clammy. We get onto Taylor Drive and cross the Red Deer River, then turn left onto Highway 11. Ahead is a cloverleaf where we might have to merge onto the QE2. I keep my eyes glued to Jeff's right-turn indicator and nothing happens. We sail across the overpass heading west.

Once we've crossed the QE2, we turn right. Burnt Park Road. It leads to an industrial district where paved lots stretch behind chain-link fences. Flat-bed trailers fill one; rows of cranes line another. No one's around at this time of night. The windowless tin buildings could be hiding anything. As we drive north, the lots turn into muddy fields, and the road changes from asphalt to dirt.

Just where the road dies out, a Range Rover SUV is waiting for us. Jeff stops his car, and I brake behind him. He gets out and motions for me to dismount. I pop the lid for him, and he lifts the bundle out. He stuffs the loose package back into place and tries to reaffix the duct tape. His hands tremble. The light is dim. The faint hum of traffic on the QE2 sounds like waves breaking in the distance.

No one has come out of the Range Rover yet.

Jeff's voice cracks. "You coming?"

It's the last thing I want to do, but we're in this together. We shuffle out from behind the Honda and inch toward the SUV. The headlights pop on, and my hands fly up to shield my eyes. Jeff's free hand does the same.

A low voice comes out the driverside window. It's as clear as a gunshot. "Drop it."

I glance at Jeff. The whites of his eyes catch the headlights. He kneels down and sets the bundle of drugs on the ground.

"Back up!"

Jeff squints, trying to see past the glare of the headlights and inside the windshield. He doesn't move. He takes a deep breath. "Where's Julie?" he calls.

The SUV's engine revs. For a split second, I'm convinced they're going to run us down. My arms and legs break into tremors. I scuttle backward and crouch beside Jeff's car. Jeff stands stock still, but his legs are shaking.

The passenger door opens, and Julie stumbles out. She rushes forward, then bends down and scoops up the package. She glances at Jeff, but her face is in a shadow. I can't read her expression. She turns and scurries back to the open passenger door. Someone yanks her inside and shuts it. Jeff is still standing there. They must be ripping open the package. What are they going to do if there's less than they thought? Keep Julie hostage?

The passenger door swings open again, and Julie falls out. It looks like she's been pushed. She stands up and brushes herself off. Then she hobbles over to us. Jeff tries to meet her halfway, but the SUV's engine roars and the headlights flash. It's pretty obvious P.A. doesn't want him to get any closer.

When Julie reaches Jeff, she's taking short, rapid breaths. "Get out. They said. We get. Head start."

"Huh?" Jeff says.

Head start? They're going to chase us?

Julie just stands there shuddering. I stand up in the lee of Jeff's car. "Come with me, Julie." I manage to unzip my backpack and pull out the helmet. Donny can't follow us where we're going to go.

Julie hasn't moved, so I dart out and grab her. Shielded by Jeff's car, I tug the helmet down over her head and snap the chin piece closed. I pull her by the hand, and she staggers behind me. When I let go of her to mount the scooter, she seems to spring back to life. She climbs on behind me. Maybe she remembers riding the scooter that other night not so long ago. The night we met Donny.

I fire up the motor and swing around, heading back down Burnt Park Road. The engine of Jeff's car starts up, too, but we beat him to Highway 11 and turn left. Merging into traffic, we lose the cars behind us. Jeff will be okay. He gave them what they wanted. All I want to do now is lose Donny before he changes his mind and comes after Julie.

And it's easy. We turn off the highway onto Taylor Drive, cross the River, and drop down to the riverside trail. It's for cyclists and pedestrians only, but I swerve between the brown metal poles on the scooter. I turn off the headlight, so no one can see us. Maybe Donny isn't even trying to follow us, but it feels much safer off road. After riding in the dark for a while, I brake at a lookout. "I think we've lost them."

"Uh-huh." Julie slides off the seat and leans on a stone wall overlooking the river. I prop up the scooter on its kickstand and follow her. Moonlight shines on the water. We stand for a long time in silence. She shivers and says, "Let's go."

"Wait." I turn to face her. "I have to ask you something."

She crosses her arms. "What?"

"How did you get involved in this in the first place?"

Her eyes flash. "You *know* how I got sucked into working for Donny."

I shake my head. The helmet makes it feel heavy. "No, I mean, why were you helping Jeff deal in the first place?"

She half laughs. "Why do you think?"

I shrug.

She spreads her arms, her palms turned toward me. "I liked him, remember? And there you were, with your driver's licence and your mom who always leaves you on your own 'til midnight . . . You were moving in on him!"

I want to deny it, but she's partly right. Once upon a time, I actually thought Jeff and I might end up dating — whether it hurt Julie's feelings or not.

"So, I had to make myself more useful to him than you were." She fiddles with the chin strap of the helmet. "Ha! Like that worked out. It all spiralled out of control after that."

We listen to the river rush by. The current dances and races away, away, across the city and east toward Saskatchewan. The rest of my questions don't seem to matter anymore. "Where should we go now?"

"Your place." She smirks. "That's where my parents think I am already."

"Really?! How'd you pull that off?"

"I pretended to call your house when I was

in the bath. I shouted to my parents, 'Can I stay over at Mary's?' They stood on the other side of the bathroom door, getting me to pass messages to your mom. And I pretended to pass messages back to them."

"That worked?"

"Yeah. My parents are actually pretty shy, at least when they have to talk to English speakers. And they like your mom."

Voices carry from down the path. We climb back onto the scooter. "I just hope they didn't decide to call while we were out."

The path winds on for eight kilometres. Even though it's dark, the riverside ride through evergreens is soothing. By the time we reach the end of the path, it feels like we've put a lot of distance between us and Burnt Park Road. I merge onto residential streets and turn the headlight back on. It's not long before I'm pulling into the carport. Mom's bedroom light is already off, but she's left the outdoor light on. I lock up the scooter. I pop open the lid to the hold under the seat. I take a good look around inside it. Hard to believe it had $1,500 worth of cocaine in it an hour ago. It looks clean and innocent now.

We let ourselves in. I'm starving all of a sudden. Mom's lasagna is waiting in the fridge. The pasta, the cheese, the tomato sauce — pure comfort food. I heat up a slice for each of us. Before I've finished eating, a wave of tiredness floods me. It numbs my limbs and weighs down my eyelids. No way I'm brushing my teeth tonight. "Julie, I've got to crash. Right now."

"That's okay," she says. "I know where you keep the sleeping bag and the foamie."

I hug her goodnight. "I'm so glad you're safe."

"Me, too, Meringue." She squeezes me, then lets go. "Thanks for going out there with Jeff tonight. I get the feeling you had an influence on him. I don't think he would have done it for me."

"Yes, he would have!"

She bites her lip and gently shakes her head. "He hates me."

I sigh. "We all ended up getting turned against each other. That's been the worst part of all this."

She wipes her nose on the back of her hand. "It's over now."

I yank a Kleenex from the box on the counter and hand it to her. "Promise me it's *all* over."

She nods. "All of it. I'm never going to touch that stuff again."

17

HOSPITAL

I jolt awake from a dream about gravel pits and backhoe loaders. My phone rings again. Julie stirs on the foamie laid out next to my bed. I fumble on my bedside table for my phone. "Hello?"

It's after 2 a.m.

"Meringue. It's Lee." He gulps in a big breath. Garbled noises in the background almost drown him out.

I snap on my bedside lamp. Julie groans and pulls the sleeping bag over her eyes. "Where are you?" I say.

Between sobs, Lee struggles to speak.

"Hospital. Waiting in Emergency."

"Oh my God! Are you okay?"

He wheezes. "Jeff."

"What about Jeff?"

Julie scrunches the sleeping bag away from her face and peers at me.

"He went out to empty the garbage and never came back. I wish I'd gone out to look for him earlier, but . . ." He trails off and breaks into sobs.

I'm on my feet, getting dressed. The hospital is only two blocks from Phat Pizza. "We'll meet you there."

Julie gets dressed, and together we creep out to the carport. I don't want to wake Mom up, so I push the scooter down the driveway. We climb on and coast for a while. When we're out of earshot from the townhouse, I start up the engine. It's pitch-dark. I take side streets to Coronation Park and find the bike path. I leave my headlight on this time. It still feels so much safer to be off-road. The trail takes us all the way to Rotary Park. I cut across the parking lot by the Tim Hortons and the Super 8, and in another block we're at the hospital.

A bright-red sign directs us to the Emergency entrance. I park just outside it. Julie clutches my arm, and we walk together. We find Lee hunched over in the waiting room, elbows on his knees and head in his hands. We sink into chairs on either side of him. He looks up and takes us in.

"How is he?" Julie asks.

"I don't know. When I found him, he was all beat up. He was lying unconscious in the alley out back. I had to . . . to drag him into the back seat of his car and drive him here." Lee sucks in so much air, it sounds like he might throw up. "I thought he might be dead."

"Lee Minh?"

A nurse has appeared in front of us holding a clipboard under her arm. Lee is too stunned to react. I nudge him with my elbow, and he nods.

"Your cousin is in stable condition," she says.

"Can we see him?" I ask.

"Only family is allowed," the nurse says. She looks at me, then at Julie and Lee. "You two can go in," she says to them. I fold my arms across my chest and settle in to wait.

It's Julie who speaks up. "Meringue's as much family as I am. Can we all see him, please?"

The nurse looks past us, checking the clock. She huffs. "Alright. But make it quick."

Jeff is lying on a cot in a room that holds three other beds. His eyes are swollen shut and his nose is covered in plaster. Red marks that are going to turn into bruises show on his neck and arms. Julie and I crowd around the head of his bed. Lee stands at the foot of it.

Julie grips the corner of Jeff's pillow. When she speaks, her voice is husky. "Was it Donny?"

Jeff grunts.

"What am I supposed to tell your dad?" Lee blurts out. His face is contorted and flushed. "I can't cover for you this time, man, you're in the fucking hospital! And my dad knows where I am, I had to tell him."

"It was the guys from Edmonton, wasn't it?" I say.

Jeff grunts again. His lips are too swollen to talk.

"And why do these two know so much more than me?" Lee cries. "We're family, dude!"

"Shut up!" someone shouts from behind the next curtain. "We're trying to sleep. Take your soap opera somewhere else."

Just then Jeff's dad, Mr. Minh, shows up. His hair is mussed up, and it looks like he's thrown an overcoat over pajamas. But he's still in charge. He brushes Julie and me back from the bed and speaks in Vietnamese. Even though his son is lying there looking half-dead, he sounds angry. Lee stands frozen. His eyes widen as he listens.

Mr. Minh turns to Julie and me. "Thank you for coming to check on my son. Please, go home to your parents now. The family will take over."

Lee nods to us as we back away from the bed and leave the room. The fluorescent lights in the hallway are blinding. It feels like I've been awake for days.

EPILOGUE

School is over except for exams. For a break from studying, I take my bike out on the trails that weave all the way through the city. Cycling helps calm my mind. And it needs all the calming it can get. Maybe it's not such a bad thing that buying a car has to wait.

I fly along beside the Red Deer River and turn south. At the hospital, Jeff's dad pieced together most of the story, and Jeff confessed to the rest. When Mr. Minh told Jeff he had to give a police report on everything he'd done, Jeff called me. "They're going to grill me. I can't promise to cover for you. I think it might be better if we all went down to the station together." By that time, I wasn't keeping any secrets from Mom, so I agreed.

Coronation Park passes in a blur of leafy

trees. The bike trail follows a winding creek into Kin Canyon. The night Julie and I returned from visiting Jeff in the hospital, Mom woke up. Once Julie left the next morning, I had a lot of explaining to do. Mom was furious with all three of us and made it clear that Jeff and Julie weren't welcome at the house. She even took away my cell phone.

It was Mom's idea that I pay the fine for delivering pizza with a probationary licence. That cut into my savings. She's also not letting me borrow the scooter until I show that I'm responsible. As for selling coke, she's still trying to wrap her head around how that could have happened, even once. "I know you wanted a job to make some money and buy a car, but where was your common sense?" She blames herself for uprooting me from Vancouver, and she's been talking to my dad about whether I should move back in with him for grade twelve.

At the bottom of Kin Canyon, instead of turning around, I hang a right and head along

32nd toward Red Deer College. Julie really didn't want to turn herself in to the cops. She confessed to a priest and promised him that she'd never use or sell coke again. That felt like enough to her. But Jeff said, "How can I tell the cops the whole truth if I can't mention you? Besides, if you admit it all now, they'll go easier on you than if they find out later."

So, in the end, all three of us went down to the police station. Being shut into a room with two-way mirrors and interrogated by a pair of officers is not an experience I want to repeat. Ever. Now we're waiting to hear if we have to appear before a judge. The RCMP said the gangs won't go after us for talking, but whenever I see a big, bald guy or a fancy SUV, I break into a sweat. It kind of gets in the way of focusing on trigonometry and the conjugations of French verbs.

I pedal fast through the college campus. The last time I saw Jeff, we were travelling in opposite directions on our bikes. We braked and veered around. As we talked, he stayed bent over his handlebars, balancing, his feet in the toe clips. He said his dad took away his car keys. At work, he demoted him to cleaner. Jeff takes out the garbage, mops the floor, and cleans the toilet. If the mousetrap ever needs to be emptied, that's his job, too. "I don't care what I have to do," he said, "as long as I can still start university in the fall."

I finish the loop and head north. As I pump my legs, my nervous energy burns off, which means I should be able to concentrate tonight. Julie and I used to study together, but Mom hasn't forgiven her and Jeff yet. I've barely seen them since we gave our police report. I can't text them, either, so we've fallen out of touch. Sometimes, leaving each other behind seems like the best way to forget our mistakes and move on. Other times, I'm really lonely. Being known as a drug dealer hasn't exactly increased my popularity among the whole-some kids at school.

Lungs heaving, I pull into the carport and dismount. A cardboard box on the doorstep catches my eye. *TO MARY* is written on the outside. I rip open the box and unroll a sheet of tinfoil to find a batch of round, cream-coloured cookies. They're fluffy-looking, and when I pick one up, it's as light as a hollow egg.

Tucked between the tinfoil and the side of the box is a piece of paper. I unfold it.

Dear Meringue,

*I made these for you. They're paciencias —
Filipino meringue cookies. Eat them as you
drink your tea and they will help you study. (And,
hopefully, bring you patience, if you need it. I
know I do!!)*

*I'm not sure if I said this already, but sorry —
and thank you. For everything. xo Julie*

I can't remember the last time I got a hand-written note. It feels kind of special. Not only that, but Julie's a terrific baker, and my mouth is watering. I stick the note back inside the box and take the cookies into the kitchen.

The two of us have been through so much together. Even if we're not meant to be best friends for life, it would be comforting to share stuff with her. Like how I'm afraid to go to jail and how I never want to see a certain walrus-sized man again. Not everyone at school can relate.

Mom doesn't want Julie coming over yet, but she never said we couldn't talk. And it's only polite to say thank you for the cookies. I pick up the phone. When Julie answers, her little sisters are laughing in the background.

ACKNOWLEDGEMENTS

Richard Wagamese inspired me to return to writing this novel with his workshop, Story-Walk. Kelly Stone helped me to complete it with her online course, Time to Write. Kari Jones's feedback and Carrie Gleason's coaching pushed the story to another level. Colleen Sharpe's knowledge enhanced the depiction of Red Deer. David Boersma taught me how to make a match person. Heartfelt thanks to all of you for your generosity and wisdom. And to all the people I've been privileged to know as students: thank you for sharing glimpses into your minds and into your worlds.

ACKNOWLEDGEMENTS